WORLD BUILDER

SILVERWOOD ACADEMY
BOOK TWO

ID JOHNSON

For Shanna

CONTENTS

CAN I COME?

Rachael

THE DOOR to the staff lounge was closed. Rachael stood outside of it for several seconds, contemplating whether or not she should walk in. She could hear voices and knew that Graham, Jared, and Sammi were all in there. Tripp's voice was distinguishable, too. Not every word was understandable, but they were definitely talking about what was going on in Baltimore, so she should probably just walk in and share what Ebony had just told her, but it seemed odd. Should she knock?

Raising her hand, she intended to let it fall on the door, but it opened the second her hand came up. For a moment, she thought she'd accidentally used her telepathy, but then she saw Graham standing on the other side. He raised his eyebrows above those beautiful lavender orbs. "Oh, I was just coming to look for you."

"I was just about to knock." She giggled nervously and let her hand fall.

"Come on in." Graham pulled the door open and stepped aside, some sort of energy passing between them. It reminded Rachael of being on a first date with someone she really liked--only in this case, this was no date, and there were a ton of other people sitting around the table in the back of the room, papers and newspaper articles scattered about with various snacks and drinks interspersed.

"Have a seat, Rach," Jared said, gesturing at a chair next to where he was sitting on one end of the table.

"Thanks." She glanced around and took note of where everyone else was and saw that Marcy and Flint were also present. Sammi was only half glaring at her, which was an improvement. As Rachael sat down, Graham took the seat next to her, pulling his water bottle over from the other side of the table next to Marcy, so she assumed he'd been sitting there before.

"You need a drink or anything?" her trainer asked, a warm smile on her face.

"No, thank you." She'd always liked Marcy, even before she met her in real life.

Tripp was sitting next to Sammi, directly across from Rachael. "Did you hear from one of your friends in Baltimore?"

"Yes. Ebony, my best friend, college roommate, co-worker at Merek and Merek... she just called. Her boss, my old boss, Frank Merek... he's acting... weird." She realized most of what she'd just said had come out a little less than perfectly coherent, but she assumed they'd be able to sort it out.

"Weird how?" Sammi asked. "I know plenty of weird people that don't need paranormal intervention."

"Well, she said he was pacing a lot, muttering to himself, rubbing his neck...." That sounded more like a person having a nervous breakdown than a victim of a vampire attack.

"So?" Sammi shrugged. "What does that have to do with us?"

Graham shifted next to her, and Rachael noticed he was giving Sammi a look that might've rivaled her own glower. Rachael appreciated him sticking up for her but pretended not to notice. "His house was broken into a few days ago. I don't know all of the details, but Ebony said he was home at the time, that the perpetrators had just gotten their hands on him when the cops showed up, and they fled. I was just thinking… there have been so many attacks in Baltimore recently. Rex mentioned he saw something suspicious in one of the videos." She looked at Tripp then, and he nodded. "What if… these guys were vampires, and he's infected?"

"Did you say Frank Merek?" Flint asked, digging through a stack of what looked like police reports.

"Yeah."

The trainer nodded and pulled out a few pieces of paper held together by a staple. "Yeah, it's right here. Happened on the sixth around two in the morning. House was ransacked but nothing taken. The owner was found in a closet in the fetal position. He said the intruders had located him, one of them pulled him up by the shoulder, and then he blacked out."

"Any wounds?" Marcy wanted to know.

"Trace amounts of blood on his shirt but no notable injuries." Flint eyed the paper for a second longer before handing it over to Marcy, who was sitting next to him.

"Would there be puncture wounds?" Rachael asked.

"Not necessarily noticeable ones." Jared had his hands folded in front of his face, deep in thought. "It depends on how long the vampire had their fangs in him."

"And how deep," Sammi added.

Rachael's stomach felt queasy. The idea that Frank could be a vampire now, that he would have to be destroyed, made her light headed. "He has a family. Could they be in danger?"

"The incubation period is seventy-two hours," Marcy reminded her. Of course, Rachel knew that. She'd determined that. "If it happened at two in the morning on the sixth…."

"Then we have about nine hours." Graham folded his arms.

"I guess we're going out tonight, then." Tripp had a grin on his face that Rachael would've considered inappropriate if she didn't know him well enough to understand he meant no disrespect. Tripp liked hunting almost as much as he liked breathing.

"Can I come?" The question was out of Rachael's mouth before she even thought about what she was asking. Protocol would dictate that she wouldn't be able to go on any hunts at all for at least another six months. She'd just started her training, after all. There were plenty of students who'd been here longer than her who hadn't been yet, not a real hunt anyway. Possibly on a practice procedure.

"Are you serious?" Sammi asked, her eyebrows knit together.

"I won't get in the way. I just want to see."

"You want to see us destroy your boss?" Marcy clarified.

"Old boss. And no, I probably don't want to see that part. But I do want to see… make sure his family is okay. Hopefully, this is a false alarm." She shrugged her shoulders. Begging would do her no good.

Graham looked around the table while Sammi shook her head in a resounding vote against Rachael's proposition. The fact that anyone was even considering it made Rachael think there was something wrong with them.

"What if she gets in trouble?" Flint asked. "We haven't even introduced that class to weapons yet. And she has no powers."

"I do!" Rachael blurted, drawing everyone's eyes again. "I do have powers."

"You do?" Jared asked, his head cocked to the side.

"Yep. Watch this." Rachael concentrated on a pencil sitting in the middle of the table. She raised her hand, and with every fiber of her being, willed the pencil to come to her. After a few seconds of nothing happening, she started to get frustrated, but remembered what Dr. Mellow had said about controlling her breathing. A few more seconds passed, and Rachael was about to give up when something moved.

It wasn't the pencil, though. It was Sammi's coffee cup. It tipped over, sending coffee splashing all over her shirt and dripping into her lap. "You have got to be shitting me!" she shouted, shooting back from the table so fast she almost slammed into the wall ten feet behind her.

"Oh no!" Rachael covered her mouth with both hands. "That's not what I meant to do at all!"

Several of the others began to laugh while Tripp gathered some paper towels for his on-again/off-again flame. Graham used his own powers to right the cup and magically put the coffee back in it, all except for what had doused Sammi.

Seeing him gather liquid droplets and drop them into the container was incredibly impressive to Rachael. She'd never seen anything like that before and wondered if she'd ever be that powerful. "I'm really sorry, Sammi."

"Yeah, you might wanna stick to using your hands for the foreseeable future," the hunter suggested, tossing the sopping paper towels into the trash. "I know I'm outnumbered here, but I say hell no she's not coming."

"I vote yes." Flint was covering his mouth with his hand to hide the fact that he was still laughing. "As long as she doesn't do that to anyone else."

"I'm with Sammi," Tripp said. "Sorry, Rach. I think you're great, but it's too early."

"Marcy?" Graham asked.

"Gosh, this is hard. I am impressed that you were able to move anything at all. And I know you've been working so hard in class. But I'd hate to see anything happen to you, and even though this should be relatively easy for the rest of us in the room to handle…. I'm sorry, hon. I'm gonna have to say no for now."

"Dr. McCall?" Graham looked at Jared, and Rachael felt any hope of getting to go melt away. Even if Graham said yes, there was no chance Jared would.

Her history professor looked at her as if he was trying to determine the age of a relic found at an archeological dig. She swallowed hard, his stare beginning to penetrate her to the core. "Yeah. She should go."

Rachael's eyes widened. She hadn't been expecting that. At all.

"That means we're tied, and in the case of a tie, the senior staff member makes the decision--" Graham explained.

"Which is you," Sammi said, glaring at him.

"Which is me." Graham smiled at Rachael, and she felt her eyes bulging out of her head.

"Wait--I get to go?"

He nodded. "Yes, but keep it on the low down. No need for the other newbies to know."

"You got it. Thanks, guys." She could hardly contain her excitement at the opportunity to actually see a real hunt in person after only writing about them for so long.

"Something tells me we are going to regret this." Sammi folded her arms over the coffee spot, getting her sleeve wet. She groaned and skulked off toward the door.

"See you at midnight, Sam!" Graham called after her.

She flipped him the bird over her shoulder and kept walking.

2

FIRST HUNT

Rachael

THE RIDE to Baltimore didn't take nearly as long in the middle of the night with Graham behind the wheel as it would have if Rachael had been driving herself. She was sitting in the very back of the SUV, next to Marcy, keeping her mouth closed. She hoped that they'd just forget she was there. The fact that Sammi was still obviously irritated as she sat in front of Rachael with her arms crossed told her that was a long shot.

Frank Merek lived in a nice house in the suburbs. The community wasn't gated, but as they pulled in, there were plenty of signs that said they were being observed by the neighborhood watch and video monitoring. Neither of those precautions had helped identify who had broken into Frank's home. While Rachael knew the hunters had methods of preventing anyone from recording them thanks to a device she'd invented that manipulated video cameras, there was always a chance someone might see them.

If the police showed up, there were ways to deal with that, too. All of the team members were licensed law enforcement officers. Their badges had been unquestionable in the world she'd invented, so she assumed they'd work here, too, even though this place looked an awful lot like the real neighborhood the real Frank Merek lived in. Being back out in the world she'd lived in for so long before she'd known about vampires was confusing.

Rachael just hoped they were able to get in, get out, and not have to answer to anyone. She usually wrote her plots that way. It was easier if the rest of the world never caught on to the hunters. But she hadn't written this, so there was no way to know what was about to happen.

Graham stopped the SUV a couple of blocks from Frank's house. Rachael had been there a few times for company parties. She recalled his bedroom was on the second story, in the far left corner of the house. His wife, Penny, was likely home, as well as their two kids. If Frank was in the bedroom, as he should be, it would be difficult to get him without waking Penny.

They didn't intend to take him out, though, not necessarily. They'd have to see if he'd been infected or not. Hopefully, he was fine, and it was just stress causing him to act so unusual at work. Rachael had a feeling in her gut that wasn't the case though. If Frank couldn't pass the tests the team would put him through, they'd be forced to destroy him. There was no such thing as a good vampire.

The team double-checked their weapons and then silently stepped out of the van. Rachael followed. Graham had spoken to her briefly before they loaded up, saying he didn't want to leave her alone in the vehicle, so she'd go along with them but stay outside. Normally, whenever an observer went on a hunt, the team left someone with them to keep them safe, but he hadn't mentioned the plan for that yet.

She followed along with Marcy and Flint behind her. The hairs on her arms were standing on end as she contemplated exactly what she'd gotten into. This was a real vampire hunt! Rachael was actually walking along beside a team of vampire hunters on the way to potentially destroy a bloodsucker.

Having worked together for years, the team moved in on the house silently, not needing to speak to each other in order to get into position. They had ear pieces that allowed them to communicate when necessary, though. They also had body cams, and Graham had installed an app on Rachael's phone that would allow her to watch.

Most of the team dispersed in different directions, leaving Rachael with Graham and Jared near the front driveway. Jared steered them over toward some high shrubs, and Rachael went along as chatter started on the earpiece. She had been instructed not to say a word unless she was in imminent danger, so she just listened as the other teammates scoped out the residence. Sammi and Tripp were already inside, having disabled the alarm and finding an unlocked window in the back of the house. Marcy was on the roof, and Flint was covering the back door.

"All right, Rach. You should be fine right here," Graham said, surveying the area. If any of the neighbors were on watch, they were doing a piss poor job as no one had raised an alarm.

Her hands were shaking as she slid back into the shrubbery a bit. "Okay." She wished she had a gun or something... just in case.

Sammi's voice came through the earpiece. "Master is clear." She took that to mean Frank wasn't in his bedroom. Where was he?

"I've gotta go." Graham was in a hurry to get in there. She could see him itching to rush off. He looked Rachael in the eyes and smiled. "See you in a few."

She nodded, unable to find any words. Was he really leaving her here alone? She'd be fine--Frank wouldn't hurt her, would he?

Graham patted her gently on the arm, nodded at Jared, and then headed off toward the house.

Rachael followed him with her eyes for a moment before she realized Jared wasn't moving. "Are you...?"

"Staying? Yeah. We couldn't leave you alone."

"You drew the short straw?" she asked, only half kidding.

Dr. McCall smirked. "Nope. I volunteered."

Rachael's eyes bulged. In her ear, she heard Tripp's voice. "Basement. Den. Second door on the left. Lock and load."

"Lock and load?" Rachael whispered, not even having had a chance to respond to Jared's confession yet. "Why would they...?"

"You know what that means, don't you Rach?" He took a step closer to her, but not in an intimidating way. His eyes were wide with fascination. "You know a lot more about all of this than you're letting on, right?"

She swallowed hard. "I'm not sure I know what you're talking about."

A grin cracked his face as he slowly shook his head. "Sure you don't. If you want to actually watch any of this, better get your phone out. It'll be over soon."

Rachael didn't want to watch them destroy her old boss, but she was also compelled to look, sort of like driving past a bad car wreck. She pulled her phone out of her pocket and opened the app, choosing to watch from Tripp's angle because he was the closest one to the location he'd just sent in. He'd be the first to make contact.

As the door to the den swung open, Rachael held her breath, preparing to watch something she knew she'd never be able to unsee.

3

———

HE'S A VAMPIRE

Rachael

TRIPP FLUNG the door to the den open violently, his weapon drawn in front of him. He had a revolver pointed at Frank. That wouldn't kill him if he was a vampire, but it would slow him down so they could more easily get a stake in his heart. At the moment, Rachael wished she'd made it easier for vampires to die and harder for hunters to. There was nothing stopping Frank from fighting back or even turning the hunters, if he was strong enough.

From the looks of it, he was. By Graham's calculations, if Frank was going to turn, it should've been in the last few minutes. Her former boss was standing near his desk, his button-down shirt open revealing a classic dad bod, but that wasn't the part that truly caught her attention. It was the two inch fangs protruding from his open mouth as he hissed at the intruder.

"Frank Merek! Don't move!" Tripp called as the vampire's hiss became a roar. The vampire swung his arms around, knocking every-thing off his desk and into the air. Pens, paper weights, photographs, a pair of scissors, everything went flying, some of it toward Tripp's head.

He fired his weapon, but in the chaos, he missed. Rachael heard nothing since she'd invented a built-in silencer that actually kept the gun from making any noise at all, but she saw Tripp's trigger finger move before he dodged out of the way.

There was only one exit since the den had no windows. Frank would have to go through Tripp to get out. The hunter wasn't alone now, though. Rachael heard footsteps flying up behind him and instinctively switched to Graham's camera.

He was there. In the hall, closing in on the door. Just as he drew his weapon, Tripp went flying out of the den, slamming into the wall across the hall from the open door. With no time to check on him, Graham raised his weapon as Frank stepped through, another roar vibrating through the basement. That one, Rachael could hear with her own ears.

Graham fired. This time, Frank wasn't so lucky. The bullet struck him in the right shoulder. He careened back into the wall as Graham fired again, hitting him in the head this time. The monster who used to be an accountant growled, staggering for a few steps before he sank to his knees.

Tripp was up now. He signaled for Graham to hold his fire as he pulled his stake out of the interior pocket of his jacket. It didn't take much for him to overpower the new vampire. He pressed him to the floor, his knees on his chest, and plunged the silver-tipped stake into Frank's heart.

Frank convulsed for a moment, his arms flailing as he attempted to free himself from Tripp's grip. Sammi pushed past Graham, but she stopped short of trying to help Tripp. He didn't need it. In another second, Frank stopped moving altogether. He was gone.

Tripp was breathing heavily as Sammi stepped forward to haul him to his feet. "Are you okay?" she asked him.

Rubbing the back of his head, Tripp said, "Yeah. Just a bit of a headache, that's all."

"Nice work," Graham said, shaking Tripp's hand. "Let's get this mess cleaned up and staged so we can get out of here."

That was enough for Rachael. As a matter of fact, she was shocked she'd watched that long. As they started to work together to make it look as if Frank had somehow died of natural causes, she turned her phone off and put it in her pocket, just now realizing she had tears streaking her cheeks.

"Are you okay?" Jared asked, his hand on her back.

"I'm okay. It's just… Frank was a good person. He never deserved to have this happen to him." She held back the part that she felt like it was her fault. Not just because she'd tipped the team off but also because she'd invented this crazy world, after all.

"It's all right," Jared said softly, pulling her to him.

Rachael rested her face on his shoulder, doing her best to stop her tears. There was no time for crying in vampire hunting, even if it was someone she knew. She thought back to the night Chell died. None of her teammates had cried until later. They'd had work to do. While this job was all but done, she needed to get her act together.

She then realized Jared was holding her a little too closely than she would've expected. She took a deep breath and inhaled his cologne--a whisper of sage and bergamot. One hand slid up her back to her hair, the other was still around her waist. "It's all right, Rachael. It's not your fault." The warmth from his breath caressed her cheek, and then she felt his warm lips on the top of her head.

Rachael lifted her eyes, not sure what to make of all of this, but in the moment, her emotions flooded, her mind became overwhelmed. When Jared lowered his face slightly toward hers, she found herself rising to meet him. His mouth was warm as it surrounded hers, and she felt herself surrendering to the calmness his touch conveyed.

It only lasted a few seconds, and when she pulled back, her eyes large with wonder, she saw confusion on her professor's face as well, as if he wasn't able to explain what had overcome him.

Then she registered the small sigh that had come from her left, and she realized they weren't alone. Graham was there, his expression conveying a wealth of emotions--disappointment, confusion, anger.

He said, "They're wrapping up. We can head back to the SUV," and turned to walk that way.

Jared had released her as soon as he realized Graham was standing there. Now, he turned around, "Shit," he muttered under his breath.

"You can say that again," Rachael concurred, looking at her history professor with wide eyes. "What the hell just happened, Jared?" Calling him Dr. McCall at the moment seemed out of the question.

"I don't know, Rach. I'm sorry. I shouldn't have…." He dropped his head, nothing more to say.

She shouldn't have either. But she had. What's more, she'd liked it.

But Graham hadn't, which made it all the more confusing. Why had he been so upset that Jared had kissed her? Did he really have feelings for her?

As the rest of the team filed out of Frank's house in silence, Rachael fell in step with them, her heart pounding in her chest. She had a lot to think about….

4

COMPLICATIONS

Graham

GRAHAM GUIDED the SUV back to the academy without a word. Normally, he'd take this time on the ride home to talk about the hunt, to review anything that had gone wrong and talk about what the team had done right. It saved him time on the reports he filed every morning after if he already had an idea of what his teammates had experienced. But tonight, he didn't feel like talking.

The rest of the team was fairly silent as well. He imagined it was out of respect for Rachael. It was different when the vampire they'd just eradicated was a known entity, and in this case, it was someone she knew well. She was clearly still distraught, sitting in the far back of the SUV, sniffling every once in a while. Graham caught a glimpse of her in the rearview mirror now and again and wished he could do something to make her feel better, but he knew there was nothing he could do.

Not that that had stopped Jared from trying.

Dr. McCall was in the passenger seat to Graham's left as he almost always was, but he was staring out the window at the nothingness the dark of night displayed. As Graham drove, he went over every conversation he'd had with Jared about Rachael since she'd started at the academy. He'd seemed fascinated with her lineage, but that hadn't transferred to anything else, not to Graham anyway. Now, he realized he'd been grossly misinterpreting the professor's intentions.

Or had he? Was it possible Jared hadn't even realized he had feelings for Rachael until they'd manifested in that kiss?

Graham felt guilty for even witnessing it, not that he'd meant to. He'd rushed up from the basement to make sure Rachael was okay. He hadn't been expecting to see Jared taking care of her so... personally. How could he possibly be mad, though? Rachael didn't belong to him. As a matter of fact, it was ridiculous to even think about dating her. Chell hadn't been gone nearly long enough to think about seeing anyone else. Yet, he'd be lying if he tried to deny the fact that Rachael had filled his thoughts almost every second since he'd first met her. Exactly why, he couldn't say. There was just some innate quality Rachael had like no one he'd ever met before that kept his mind occupied with thoughts of her even when he should've been doing something else... anything else.

They arrived back at campus a little before 4:00 in the morning. The sun would be coming up soon. Most of the team was used to sleeping odd hours, but he had a feeling Rachael wasn't. She would probably sleep most of the day. Luckily, it was the weekend, so she didn't have any classes. Hunting all night and then trying to work or go to class the next day sucked, so they all tried to avoid it when they could. Sometimes it couldn't be helped.

The team piled out of the car without much chit chat. Marcy said to Rachael, "Come on, girly. I'll walk you home." The trainer wrapped her arm around Rachael's shoulders and started to walk her back to the dorm building, but he caught Rachael's eyes for just a split second as she went. He fought the urge to tell Marcy he'd walk her. It was evident Rachael had something she wanted to say to him, but now wasn't the time.

"Graham, can we talk?"

So now Jared wanted to speak to him. Everyone else was gone, and Graham was about to hang up the keys to the SUV on the peg where they kept the keys to all of the academy vehicles. Thoughts of going home, drinking too much, and sleeping it off, sounded much more appealing than talking to Jared about anything.

But it was better to get it out in the open now. "Sure." They were alone in the garage now, everyone else having scattered as soon as they came to a stop. Whether someone had seen what he had in real life through his body cam video or they were just that intuitive, he couldn't say, but it was probably best to get this over with now, while the two of them were alone.

Jared took a deep breath, his hands in his pockets. "I'm sorry, man. I don't know what happened. I didn't plan that."

"Why are you apologizing to me? Rachael's not... mine."

"I know that. But the two of you seem to be getting pretty close. I'm not saying that I think you're ready to move on or anything, but you do like her, don't you?"

Graham shrugged. "I guess I haven't really thought about it. Rachael's cool." His acting wasn't that good. Jared saw right through him.

"Look, I haven't mentioned this to anyone else, but I think there's something really special about her, something we might not quite understand. I've been doing my best to figure out what it is, and I think she knows more than she's saying. At the same time, the more I'm around her, the more I'm drawn to her. I don't like it--I'm her teacher for Christ's sake."

"And yet you kissed her." Graham was stating the obvious, and it came out rude, but at the moment he didn't care. The leather they wore on the hunts in an attempt to keep the vampire's claws from penetrating their skin was growing warmer by the minute. He was ready to take his jacket off and hang it up for a while.

"I did. But I didn't mean to. And it wasn't...."

"Wasn't what? Good? What you were expecting? Enough tongue?"

"Graham...."

"What? Jared, what do you want me to say? You can kiss her if you want to. Hell, you can sleep with her if you want to. She's not mine." A pang in his stomach fired off, and Graham turned to take the keys over to the hook to hide the nausea his own statement had induced.

"I was going to say I don't think she would've kissed me back if she hadn't been so emotional about Frank. It wasn't real. It was just one of those things that happens in the heat of the moment."

Graham placed the keys on the hook and turned back to face his friend. "But you weren't overly emotional, not about the hunt, anyway. Were you?"

Jared shook his head. "No. I kissed her because I wanted to. I'm sorry."

"Don't be sorry to me, man. You do what you want."

"Graham, that's bullshit and we both know it. If Chell hadn't just passed away…."

Graham froze and looked at his friend. "What? If Chell was still alive, do you think I'd be breaking up with her to go after Rachael?"

"No, that's not what I meant. But if it was a year ago, or if you and Chell had never been a couple, wouldn't you be more willing to show your attraction to Rachael?"

Running a hand through his hair, Graham shrugged. "Hell, Jared, I don't know. It doesn't matter. Chell did die recently. And she was my fiancée. So, beyond that, it probably doesn't matter."

Jared took a few steps closer to Graham so he could look him in the eyes. "I just don't want there to be anything between us, man. You're one of my best friends, maybe my best friend. If you want me to stay away from her, I will."

"I don't want you to do anything for me, Jared. If you like her then I'm not gonna stand in your way."

The professor nodded. "You're not going to be able to stay away from her yourself though, are you?"

Shrugging, Graham said, "I have no fucking idea, Dr. McCall. I can try. But I won't make any promises."

Jared snickered. "Oh, good. A love triangle. What I've always wanted."

"I wouldn't call it that. Maybe an infatuation triangle." Graham was done talking about all of it. That beer was calling his name. "Have a good night, Doc." He patted his friend on the shoulder and took off, not wanting to walk back to the dorms with him or anyone else. Graham just wanted to be alone--unless he could be with Rachael instead. Since that wasn't an option at the moment, he'd have to settle for his own company for the foreseeable future.

5

FILLING THEM IN

Rachael

THE SOUND of her phone vibrating had been ignorable--but the knocking on her door was too much, and Rachael finally managed to haul herself up out of bed, pulling her sleep mask off and grabbing for her robe as she stumbled to the door. She prayed it wasn't a guy because she was pretty sure she looked like hell.

"Who is it--and why do you want to die?" she asked before she even got to the peephole.

A giggle on the other side answered her question. "Woman, it's past noon!" Jazz's familiar voice called through the door.

Pulling the door open, Rachael said, "So what? I didn't get home until 4:00 and didn't fall asleep until almost 6:00." She left the door open for the woman-child to come in and slunk back to her bed. Jazz closed the door and followed as Rachael collapsed, not wanting to adult at all that day, especially after she remembered everything that had happened the night before.

Jazz plopped down on the bed, popping Rachael up into the air.

She grumbled a curse word and glared at the girl. "So… how did it go? They got him, huh?"

"Yeah. They did." Jazz was the only one she'd told about the hunt, not because she'd wanted to but because she'd seen her leaving to join the rest of the team in the middle of the night. She couldn't otherwise explain her hunting garb or the fact that she was going out when she should've been fast asleep.

"Sorry. That must've been rough."

Rachael thought about how awful it was to see them kill Frank and closed her eyes. She didn't even know what fabrications they'd put in place so that it wouldn't look like he was a vampire, but she imagined it had taken a lot of magic to hide a bullet hole--and fangs. She'd given those abilities to several team members, but Marcy was the queen. "It wasn't good."

"Well, it's really cool you got to go, even if it was someone you know, which sucks. At least he won't be sucking anymore."

Rachael shook her head at the lame, ill-timed joke. "I'm pretty sure he didn't get that far."

"You wanna go grab some lunch?"

"Not now. I'm still asleep."

"My stomach's rumbling. I'm going now." Jazz hopped up off the bed. "It's gonna be hard for me not to tell anyone about this, you know."

"You promised, Jazz. No one. Not even Rex."

"I will do my best. Maybe you should get up and stop me."

Instead, Rachael threw a pillow at her. Jazz's reflexes were good, though, and she caught it. "That all you got, woman?"

"No, I got more. But I'm asleep." Rachael considered picking up all of the pillows with her abilities and flinging them at her, but the way her luck was going, she'd accidentally throw the TV or her laptop.

"See you, Ray Ray."

Rachael groaned again, remembering that's what Tony called her, and headed to take a shower.

When she got out, she saw that she had several missed calls from Ebony, a text, and a voicemail. Clearly, her friend was upset about

Frank. Now that she was somewhat coherent, Rachael called her back. "Hey, I heard about Frank," she said quietly.

"Can you believe that? A heart attack at fifty-two? I feel so terrible, Rach. I thought there was something wrong with him, but I had no idea it was this!"

"I know Ebony, but you did everything you could."

"I should've driven him to the doctor myself."

"The way he was acting, that wouldn't have been safe."

"I've never heard of anyone acting so irrationally before they have a heart attack, though, have you? His wife said he was so irritable all night, she took the kids and went to a hotel."

"I didn't realize that." It was good to know that the house was actually empty the night before. She guessed when they'd said her bedroom was clear, they really meant clear. She'd assumed they meant clear of vampires. "It's all just awful, Eb. Maybe you should take some time off, go visit your mom."

"I am. The whole company is closing down for two weeks for bereavement. They asked us to come in in the morning and let all of our clients know we'd be working on accounts remotely but only handling problems that can't wait."

Rachael wanted to sigh in relief. Ebony's mom had moved to Florida a few years ago. It should be relatively safe, especially if Sasha hadn't chosen Frank by accident and was potentially closing in on people Rachael knew. She'd been worried about her own family recently. She needed to talk to Graham about that. Or maybe Jared....

"Rach, did you hear me?"

"Yeah, I did. I'm sorry. I was just thinking about Frank. I'm glad you're able to take some time."

"Me, too. This whole city seems to be going crazy right now with all of these break ins and murders. It's insane. Your mom has an alarm, doesn't she?"

"Yes. I got it for her a couple of Christmases ago. Besides, she doesn't live in the city."

"It doesn't seem to matter. They're hitting people in the suburbs, too. You got good security at that college of yours?"

"We do--the best."

"Good. Guess I won't worry about you then."

Rachael smiled. If she only knew. "All right, Eb. Take care, girl, and keep me up to date."

"Will do."

"I love you."

"Love you, too. Rach."

Rachael hung up and took a few deep breaths. This was all getting very real. Surely, Sasha wasn't aware of who she was or what she could do, was she?

Her phone chimed again and she looked down to see a text from Jared. "Can I talk to you?"

"Ugh." That was something she didn't even know how to respond to. Since her stomach was roaring, she decided to go eat something first and then deal with Dr. McCall. Things were getting complicated....

6

HE DOESN'T STOP

Rachael

THE CAFETERIA WAS full of students eating lunch. Rachael didn't have any choice but to sit with some of the other Lower Summer students she knew, even though she would've rather eaten alone. Jazz was still there when she came in, but she was sitting with some older guy she didn't know and some of his friends. So, she sat with Karma, Tony, and a few other people from some of her classes.

Conversing was not her forte that day. In fact, she was having trouble paying attention to what they were talking about. Her mind was elsewhere. Thoughts of Frank's poor family, what was happening with Ebony and the rest of the staff of Merek and Merek, and what Sasha was up to kept her distracted.

She was just about done with her lunch when she happened to look over and see Jared walking toward her. Rachael sucked in a deep breath. She hadn't checked her phone recently, but she had a feeling he'd probably called or sent her more texts.

"Dr. McCall!" Karma said, with a big smile. "How are you? We heard you went on a hunt last night. Did you get the vampire?"

He looked at Rachael, and she shook her head slowly to let him know they hadn't heard a thing from her.

"We did," Jared said with a small smile. "How are all of you doing this afternoon?"

"Good. Got to get back to the room and study for that quiz tomorrow." Tony chuckled, as if it was an inside joke.

"It'll be fine," Jared assured him.

"Easy for you to say. You wrote the test!" Tony thought that was hilarious, and the other students at the table laughed politely, except for Rachael. She smiled but couldn't bring herself to laugh.

"Rachael, can I talk to you for a minute?" Jared asked as soon as he was done contributing to the polite laughter.

She raised an eyebrow. Was he really going to do this now? She could hardly say no, so she stood and walked a few steps away from the table with him. Trying to keep a pleasant expression on her face for the sake of the others, she asked, "Yes?"

"Hi."

"Hi...."

"I was hoping you'd call me back."

"Well, I've been here for almost an hour. So...."

"Will you go for a ride with me? There's something I want to show you."

Swallowing hard, she looked back at the table. They were chatting, but every student had one eye on her and the professor. Tony had two. "Uh... well, I have a history quiz to study for."

"You'll be fine."

"I don't know. The material's a little difficult...."

"I'll give you the answer key."

"That's cheating. I don't want to be accused of cheating."

He rolled his eyes. "Rach, it won't take long."

"Fine." She ran a hand through her hair. "Just let me put my tray away."

Jared nodded and went over to the staff table where a few other people, including Marcy and Flint, were sitting.

"Everything okay, Rachael?" Karma asked. She genuinely looked concerned.

"Oh, yeah. Everything's fine. But I'm gonna go."

"With Doc?" Tony asked, arching an eyebrow.

"Yeah. He just wants to talk to me about… class."

They weren't buying it. "Okay, well, text me if you need anything." Karma looked concerned, and Rachael could only imagine what they thought was going on.

"Will do." Rachael forced a smile, trying to assure them everything was fine, though she wasn't sure of that herself.

"We're going to get together to study for the quiz in a little while," Tony added. "Come on over when you're done talking to the prof."

"Sure." Rachael picked up her tray and headed across the room to dump it, not planning on taking him up on the offer. She had already read the chapter and knew she'd do fine on the quiz, and she'd rather not spend her time with people who didn't know what had gone on the night before. It was hard to pretend she hadn't watched a man she really liked kill her former boss--oh, and kissed her professor.

Jared walked out of the cafeteria ahead of her but was waiting in the hallway. She imagined that was for the other staff members' sakes.

Silently, she followed him out the door and walked across the yard with him toward the garage. He drove a sensible sedan, a gray Audi A3. His car of choice stood in stark contrast to Graham's flashy sports car.

He opened the passenger side door, and Rachael got in, wondering where he was taking her. She knew him well enough not to question her safety, but it was still odd to her to be getting in the car with one of her college professors she'd only technically known for a few weeks.

Once they were through the gates, Jared said, "Thanks for agreeing to come with me, Rachael."

"Sure." As if she had a choice…. "Can you tell me where we're going?"

"You'll see in a minute."

She considered pushing it, but didn't. After a few turns down country roads, she figured it out anyway. Rachael took a deep breath and tried to stay calm. What in the world was his point in taking her out here?

About five minutes after she'd gotten into the car, Jared pulled over outside an old wrought iron gate that was more decorative than protective. He came around and opened her door, and Rachael stepped out. "Welcome to Pleasant Grove Cemetery." He offered her his hand, but she didn't take it. Whatever his point was, it better be good.

7

———

CEMETERY

THE CEMETERY WAS PEACEFUL. Even in the afternoon sun, there was a gentle breeze that stirred the leaves of the shade trees planted intermittently between the tombstones. The grass was green and freshly mowed. The name Pleasant Grove seemed fitting from an aesthetic viewpoint, though she didn't think there was anything pleasant about the prospect of what was lying beneath the tombstone Jared led her to.

Rachael had invented this place. She knew that, if she wandered around long enough, she'd see lots of other grave markers for various vampire hunters who had come through the academy, including Graham Silverwood himself, the founder and ancestor of Graham Halloway. Older grave markers lined the back part of the cemetery. Rachael had always been fascinated by the artistry that went into some of the sculptures and inscriptions.

That wasn't what Jared had brought her here to see, though. She was standing in front of a fairly fresh grave. The tombstone said simply, "Chell Knight, January 17, 1995 - May 2, 2020." Rachael stared at it for a long moment, not sure what to say. It wasn't yet clear

29

to her why Jared had brought her here, but she assumed he'd explain if she waited long enough.

It took Jared several minutes to say anything at all. When he did, it was vague, and Rachael had trouble discerning his purpose. "One life affects so many others, often in ways we can't even fathom, until something changes, and the catalyst is discovered."

Rachael raised an eyebrow, hoping he'd say more because she wasn't following. When he didn't, she said, "Everyone loved her."

"Yes. She even had meaning in the lives of people who never met her in person. Like you. But then... I wouldn't say you didn't know her just because you never met her."

Starting to catch on to his meaning, Rachael asked, "What are you trying to say, Jared?"

"I'm saying... I think you know Chell in ways the rest of us didn't. I think... somehow, you're connected to us, and that you know how. But you're not saying."

Racheal was shaking her head before he even finished. "I don't know what you're talking about, Jared."

"I think you do. You're afraid if we find out, though, we'll all hate you."

Pressing her hand to her forehead, Rachael backed away from the grave. There was a bench beneath a tree several yards away. She went there and sat down, trying to decide whether or not now was the time to come clean. Could she trust him enough to tell him the truth?

Jared sat down next to her. "One of the theories in the book our grandfathers worked on together is that there are certain people who are capable of causing two worlds to come together--not to actually collide, but to sort of, overlap. He called these people "scribes" because it was through the power of their words that they brought two realities together. He didn't think this happened often, possibly only a few times in the history of our current reality, but he did think that's how vampires came to exist on our plane, long ago, back in the times of Vlad the Impaler. In your reality, there were no vampires until a few weeks ago--when you brought your reality and ours together."

She stared at him for a moment. He seemed to be much further ahead of her when it came to detangling what had happened. How could she argue with that? "But Jared... how is that possible? There was no magic in my life up until the day Graham knocked on my door."

"There was magic--but it was docile and only embodied within a few special souls. I think your grandfather was one of them, and that's why my grandfather chose him to help with the book."

"But... if what you're saying is accurate, the Wesley Barnes that knew Wadsworth McCall wouldn't have been my grandfather--he would've been your reality's version of Wesley Barnes."

Jared was shaking his head before she finished. "I don't think so. I think he realm-hopped. I think he had a different sort of magic altogether, that your grandfather came into our world and then went back. I think you could've done that, too, but instead, your power was great enough that you actually brought the worlds together."

"So I just happened to start writing about a world my grandfather visited decades ago? And managed to get all of the details correct? Through, what? Lucky guesses?"

"No. I think you had a guide, otherwise known as a muse, from this realm helping you, even though you didn't know it."

Rachael ran a hand through her hair, her fingers getting tangled in the end. She pulled them loose and took a few strands with her. Frustrated, she shook them off. "Who, Jared? Have you been whispering in my ear at night? Telling me what to write?"

"Not me. And I'm pretty sure that's not how it works. How old were you when your father left?"

"What in the world does that have to do with anything?" She was starting to get angry now.

"Just tell me. How old were you?"

"I don't remember exactly. Not very old."

"Your mom thought he just disappeared, right?"

"Yeah, so? He left and never came back. Never called. Fell off the face of the earth."

"Did anyone in your family ever see him or speak to him?"

She shrugged. "I think my grandparents did."

Nodding, Jared said, "Your grandpa?"

"Would you please tell me what you're getting at!"

"Rachael, I don't think your dad left you on purpose. I think, somehow, he realm-hopped. He's either stuck here or stuck somewhere that you can only get to from here. Which means, in order to get out, he needed someone to bring these two worlds together."

Her head was starting to hurt. Everything Jared was saying seemed absolutely ridiculous and impossible. Yet, here she was in a cemetery full of vampire hunters, including those whose stories she had written, whose deaths she had brought to fruition.

Unless what Jared was saying was true. Then, she wasn't actually making things happen. She was simply telling what had already happened in this reality.

"How did I get here, then?"

"You wrote yourself in, remember? That's what brought the two worlds together."

"But they didn't happen at the same time. I didn't put myself in the story at the same time as I actually spoke to you in the hallway."

"No, you wouldn't have to. Time doesn't work that way. It's not a continuum."

"You're about to make my head explode, Dr. McCall."

He raised an eyebrow. "Dr. McCall? Really?"

"Well, when you sound like that...."

Jared shook his head. "Rachael, what I'm telling you, is I don't think you're responsible for this." He gestured at Chell's grave in the distance. "Come on. There's one more thing I want to show you."

He took her hand and gently pulled her up off the bench. Rachael wondered where they might be going now, but she had so much to think about, she couldn't do anything other than follow him.

8

ANOTHER STOP

Rachael

"WHERE ARE WE GOING?" It wasn't the first time she'd asked the question that afternoon, and it wasn't the first time Jared refused to answer. He had driven through Waynesboro and kept on driving. Soon, she saw they were crossing over into Maryland. "Jared?"

"You'll see."

"You said that last time. You also said it wouldn't take long last time."

"That was before I decided I wanted you to see this, too."

"What is it?"

He didn't answer, and she blew out a hot breath in frustration. Running her hands through her hair, she cursed herself for ever leaving home without her history notes. "Can we at least study for my history quiz while I drive? I can't afford to get a bad grade."

"Relax. You have a perfect score at the moment."

"Still…"

"Okay. What year did the vampire attack on Roanoke take place?"

"That's easy. That's just regular history. 1590."

"It's on the quiz."

"Then you must give super easy quizzes."

He rolled his eyes at her. "What are three reasons for the vampire invasion of France in 1789?"

Equally as easily, Rachael answered, "Ready food supply from the *Bourgeois* and lower classes, lack of leadership from the monarchy, and a chaotic economic system."

"See, you'll do fine."

Rachael folded her arms, not convinced. Just because she'd gotten two easy questions right, that didn't mean she was going to ace the quiz.

He pulled off the highway into Hagerstown, Maryland. Rachael still had no idea where they were going. She remembered writing a few vampire hunts that took place here but nothing more.

A few minutes later, Jared pulled the car over in front of a large Queen Anne home. It was beautiful, but a little run down, and it looked like the yard could use a good mowing. "Guess the neighbor boy is absconding with my money without providing lawn care services," Jared muttered. He opened his door, and Rachael did the same, still unsure where they were.

She followed him up the walkway onto a porch that sagged in a few places. He didn't knock. Instead, he opened the door and shouted, "Grandma?"

"Grandma?" Rachael repeated. He'd taken her to his grandma's house? "No offense, Dr. McCall, but I don't think I'm ready to meet your family."

He rolled his eyes at her. "Darn. And I just bought the ring."

"Jared, honey, is that you?" The voice that came from the back of the house sounded sweet--and old. A white head appeared in the hall-way, followed by the body of a hunched over woman who walked about as fast as Scrappy when Rachael used her "you're in trouble" voice.

"Hi, Grandma." Jared kissed her on the cheek and gave her a gentle squeeze. "How are you?"

"Good, good. I was just bakin' some cookies for your sister's kids.

They's supposed to come over after church. Now, who is this young lady. You didn't tell me you was seein' somebody. And she's so pretty too!"

Rachael felt her face go red. "Hello, Mrs. McCall. I'm Rachael Barnes. I'm a new... hunter at the academy." She didn't think the grandmother needed to hear her grandson was having social visits with students. Rachael waved, but Grandma wanted more.

"Aren't you precious!" She pushed past Jared and gave Rachael a hug. While it should've seemed odd, she was so sweet, and smelled like cookies, Rachael couldn't *not* hug her back. It had been a long time since an old person had hugged her, and she remembered how therapeutic it could be. "Now, what brings you by, honey?" she asked, turning to Jared.

"I need to show Rachael something in the office."

"Now, you know Grandpa didn't like anyone messing with his personal items, dear."

"I know, Grandma. But this is Rachael Barnes. Wesley's grand-daughter."

"Oooh." She nodded--that was different. "Well, I'll be. I was so sorry to hear about his passing. He was such a good man."

"Thank you. We were all... very sad." Behind his grandmother's back, Jared shook his head in disbelief, and Rachael narrowed her eyes at him. She could be sad that her grandpa that she hadn't seen in twenty years had died.

"Maybe the cookies will be done by the time you're finished," Grandma said as Jared took Rachael by the wrist and walked her back toward the stairs.

"I sure hope so," he called. Then, to Rachael, he said, "Grandma makes the best cookies."

"Smells like it."

Once he had her headed the right direction, he could've let go of her. But he didn't. Instead, he slipped his hand down so that he was holding hers. Rachael wasn't sure what to think of that, but she didn't say anything. And she didn't pull away.

Jared opened a door at the end of the hall. It squealed in protest, as if it also didn't want to be disturbed. The scent of mildew and old papers was overwhelming. She also picked up on the scent of chalk, and when she walked in, she realized why. "Good gravy," she muttered.

The office was large, with a desk as big as Rachael's bed in the middle. Stacks of papers and books covered the entire surface so that she couldn't even see that there was a chair behind it until after she took a few steps into the room. One wall was covered in bookshelves that reached the ceiling, which had to be ten feet tall. The other three walls were lined with chalkboards--except for the three windows in the room and the door.

Every surface of the chalkboards was covered in math problems, diagrams, and writing she could hardly decipher. "What is all of this?"

"Grandpa's findings." Jared walked over to a filing cabinet wedged between the bookshelves and pulled out the third drawer. He dug around for a few seconds before he pulled out a rolled up tub of paper. Since the desk was occupied, he dropped down onto a large rug in the center of the wooden floor and unrolled the paper.

The diagram on the paper was similar to the ones on the chalkboard, but this one had an answer. Rachael had no idea what any of it meant. The figures and drawings--spheres colliding, stick figures, triangles. She sat down next to him, leaning over his shoulder, her knee against his thigh, ignoring the fact that he smelled so much better than the old paper.

"See--this is the formula for the realms overlapping and morphing into one." He pointed to the paper, where two spheres were joined. "And this is his theory on how a scribe can be the catalyst, with assistance from a muse. But there's a space here, where the two worlds overlap, sort of like a Venn Diagram. I believe your dad might be caught in there somewhere. Maybe we can figure out how to get him out. And… maybe we can see if there's a way to use your scribe powers to alter our current reality to provide an alternative to Chell's death and Sasha's escape."

"But… how is that possible?" She turned her head to look at him, and he did the same. Their lips were less than an inch apart. She blinked, trying not to get distracted.

"I'm not sure, but it's that formula right there." He pointed at the chalkboard, and she turned to look. "The one without an answer."

"Do we have to solve it before we can do it?"

"Probably, but I haven't been able to figure it out."

"Great. I'm no mathematician."

Jared was facing her again. "Someone's got to know how to do it."

"Have you asked any of the other professors?"

He nodded. "Rex is good at math. Maybe he can do it."

She smirked. "If you can't do it, I don't think Rex can, but it's worth a shot." Rachael pulled out her phone and stood, glad to be free of his pull. She took a picture of the math problem and put her phone back in her pocket. But when she turned, Jared was right there.

He brushed her hair back away from her face.

"You're killin' me, Doc."

The guilty grin that took over his face was irresistible. "Sorry. Can't help it."

"You don't really seem to be trying."

He shrugged. "True." And then he kissed her.

Jared's hands came around her waist, and Rachael felt herself lifting off the ground, up on her tiptoes as her hands went around his neck. This wasn't the sweet, innocent kiss from the night before. No, this was a "screw Grandpa's hard work, I'm clearing this desk" kinda kiss that she felt all the way to the soles of her feet. Her fingers twisted in his hair, and his hands found their way beneath her T-shirt to her ribs. His touch was firm, meaningful, and she wanted him to keep going, to slide his hands higher, but he didn't. Instead, he pulled back and looked at her.

"What?" Rachael asked, quietly.

"I can't ever be Graham."

"I can't ever be Chell."

He kissed her again.

9

STUCK IN THE MIDDLE

Rachael

HER PHONE WAS VIBRATING before she even made it out of Jared's car. Rachael had a feeling that she'd missed a few texts, but she hadn't wanted to check it in front of him. Something told her that neither of them needed to be reminded that someone else wanted her time.

Jared didn't walk back to the dorm room with her, which she was thankful for. Instead, he headed to his office to get some work done. After the make-out session in his grandmother's upstairs office, they'd gone down to the kitchen for cookies and to visit with the sweet old woman who had no idea how scandalously her professor grandson had been acting just above her head. What would the academy president say if he knew that one of the professors was passionately kissing one of his students?

Actually, Rachael was pretty sure no one cared. It wasn't the first time it had happened, and it likely wouldn't be the last. It wasn't as if she wasn't an adult. Though, it did seem a little unfair to the other students. Still, she was willing to continue to put in the work it took to earn a good grade in Jared's class.

And then there was the fact that she wasn't even sure how she felt about him in the first place. Kissing him was awesome. He was really good at it. But... was she just projecting her feelings for Graham on to Jared? If she could somehow manage to bring Chell back from the dead, how would Graham feel about her then? Obviously, he'd be so happy to see his fiancée, Rachael would just be the nice girl who saved her--after having killed her. She still wasn't convinced Jared had it right with the whole "you didn't kill her, you just reported it" bit. Although, crazy lumped on top of crazy was just a bigger helping of crazy.

Back in her room, she finally checked her phone. Scrappy bumped up against her leg, begging for attention. Rachael scratched her ears as she read two texts from Graham. "Can we talk? Are you around?" followed an hour later by, "I'm really sorry for the way I acted last night. I had no right." Clearly, he thought she was mad at him for being upset at her, which would've been insane. She had no right either.

His voicemail was short. "Hey, sorry to be a pain in the ass. I was just... will you call me please? I feel really bad about the way I reacted last night. I just wasn't expecting that. Anyway, please call me. This is Graham, by the way. Halloway."

She couldn't help but laugh at his attempt at humor. Of course, she knew who it was. Unsure of exactly what she was even going to say, she dialed his number. He answered immediately. "Hi. Sorry--I was out."

"With Jared? I mean, not that it's any of my business. It's just... I couldn't find him either."

"Yes, with Jared. It's fine that you asked. I'm not mad at you. I am confused."

"Good. That makes three of us, I think."

She snickered. "Why is it good that I am also confused?"

"Well, that would be better than you just telling me to go to hell. Unless you're just confused as to why I haven't taken myself to hell yet."

Laughing, Rachael said, "No, I'm just confused as to why you care about what's going on between Jared and me. If anything is going on between us...."

"Me, too. But... I think I need to talk to you about it. I talked to him about it last night when we got back."

"You did?" Jared hadn't mentioned that. She wondered why.

"I did. But practically everything I said was a lie, so, I guess it really doesn't matter that I did. Anyway, would you mind coming over here? I don't really want to come to your apartment right now."

"Sure. I'll be there in a couple of minutes." She hung up before he could say more--in case he changed his mind.

Standing in front of the mirror, she straightened her hair and decided she needed a fresh coat of lipstick, glad she'd invested in the smudge proof kind even though it cost a little more. "What are you doing, Rach?" she asked herself. Why in the world did she care about her lipstick going to see Graham? It wasn't like he was going to kiss her, too. Who the hell did she think she was?

But he was interested in her. She knew that. He never would've acted the way he had the night before if he didn't like her. So... once she was satisfied she looked pretty damn good, she headed over to the staff side of the dorm building.

Her phone was going nuts in her pocket, but she refused to look at it. If it was Graham attempting to tell her never mind, she didn't want to know. If it was Jared trying to keep her out of Graham's room, she also didn't want to know that.

As she walked, she promised herself to keep herself in check, not to reveal too much. As much as she wanted to get it over with, he could only handle so much at a time. Yet, she also knew, once she looked into those lavender eyes, there was no telling what might come out of her mouth. Chances were, everything was about to go down right now, for better or worse. She just prayed it wasn't the worst.

1 0

EXPLAINING TO GRAHAM

Rachael

RACHAEL PUNCHED Chell's code into the door that led to the staff dorms without even thinking twice about it, and when it beeped, she made her way to Graham's room, glad no one saw her. Two quick knocks on the door, and he pulled it open.

"Hey. How did you get in? I texted you to let me know when you got here, and I'd come open the door."

She pulled her phone out of her pocket. So he had. Twice. "I, uh… someone was going out."

"And let a student in?"

She shrugged. "Hey, I'm here, all right?"

He opened the door for her, and Rachael noted he looked disheveled, like he hadn't slept the night before. Normally, his hair was perfect without a single strand out of place, but not today. He hadn't shaved, and he had circles under his eyes--not dark ones, but they were there. "Graham, what's going on?" She plopped down on his couch before he even got a chance to invite her to. He sat down on the other end. "You look--very un-Graham like."

"Thanks. It's been a long night."

Rachael tilted her head to the side and pondered him for a minute. "So… what did you want to talk to me about?"

"Uh… well… Jared said some things last night that got me thinking. For most of the night. I just wanted to tell you that, uh, I think we may have a problem. And I don't know what to do about it. But you and I are both mature adults, and I'm sure we can come up with something."

Rachael arched an eyebrow. "What is that, exactly? Graham, do you have feelings for Jared?"

She'd caught him off-guard, which is exactly what she was going for, and he couldn't help but laugh. "Yes, but not like that. Though, if I were to ever take a husband…. No." He shook his head as if trying to clear it. "We are really good friends, though. I think if I hated his guts it would be a lot easier to tell you what I'm trying to tell you."

"Why try to tell me? Why not just tell me? What do you think I'm going to do? Spill coffee all over you?"

"No, but you might think I'm a horrible person."

"What makes you think I don't already think you're a horrible person?"

"Touché."

"Graham, if you're trying to tell me you think you like me a little bit, and that scares the hell out of you, because your fiancée just passed away, and you know you're not supposed to be thinking about anyone like that, then you don't have to say any of that because I just did."

"Good. That's what I wanted to say. Now, can you tell me, 'Thank you, Mr. Halloway. I'm very flattered, but I'm desperately in love with your best friend, Dr. McCall, and while you're obviously a fetching, intelligent, strapping man, you're simply not my type.'?"

Rachael grinned at him the whole time he was talking. He sounded so ridiculous. "Is that what you want me to say?"

He shook his head. "No, but it would be easier if that's what you said."

"Sorry--can't say that."

"No?"

Rachael slid a little closer to him on the couch and put her hand on top of his. "Nope. I have no freakin' idea what's going on with me and Jared, but I do know that I like you. A lot. And I'm so very sorry about Chell. If you need time, that's fine. I totally understand that. But… I think you're pretty perfect."

Graham was quiet for so long, Rachael half expected him to tell her the whole thing was a joke, and he didn't really like her at all. Instead, he took a deep breath and said, "Well, shit."

Rachael couldn't help but laugh. "Sorry."

"No, don't be sorry. I just… don't know what to do."

"I don't either. But listen…." She scratched her head, sliding away from him again and letting go of his hand. "There are some things you should probably know. I know a lot more about this world than I've been letting on."

He raised an eyebrow. "Jared said something about that."

"Yeah, he thinks I have a muse or something that had me connected to the academy before I got here. It's complicated, but Graham, I know almost everything that's happened here, at least for the last three-ish years. Maybe it's some sort of strong family magic. Jared said he thinks my grandfather had it too, and that my dad might actually be stuck… in a different realm. I'm not sure I understand all of it. I thought… I thought I'd caused everything that happened here. But Jared doesn't think that's the case."

"Wait--caused it? What do you mean?"

She took a deep breath. As long as she was being honest, she should just go through with it. "I thought… I had written this world. Remember I told you about my book, when I first met you?"

Graham nodded his head, his eyebrows knit together.

"Well, Jared doesn't think I actually created it. He thinks I was just reporting on what was actually happening in a different realm, only, when I wrote myself into the story, I caused the two worlds to collide, like in that book his grandpa wrote, that mine helped with."

"Hold on--this whole time, you thought you invented us?"

"Yes. That's how I knew who you were. That's how I knew Chell's code to get in here."

"So you knew that was her room?"

Rachael nodded.

"And you knew that was her bedspread?"

She nodded again.

Graham's face went pale. "You... thought you were responsible for her death. And if what you're saying is true, then, you are responsible for her death."

Rachael was regretting ever opening her damn mouth. Any affection for her she'd seen in his eyes a few moments ago was gone now. "I didn't know she was real. I thought it was a book."

He ran his hands through his hair. "But... why would you want to kill her? She didn't deserve to die."

"Why? I don't know. I was just... trying to change the plot a little bit. Be unpredictable." That wasn't true though. "I hadn't planned on writing myself into the book, Graham, but when I realized that I had written myself in, before I knew any of this was real, I was glad--because when I thought I was writing you--I was writing you for me."

"For you? So... I'm, what, your perfect man?"

"Yeah."

"And Chell was...."

"Who I'd want to be if I could be anyone in the world."

"Up until the point when that vampire slashed her throat, I guess."

"I'm sorry, Graham. I didn't mean to do that.... I didn't mean to do it to a real person."

"But she was a real person, Rachael. And so am I. I'm not exactly sure what you are right now, though."

"You're telling me," she muttered. Rachael got up. "I'm sorry. I shouldn't have said anything until I knew for sure what had happened."

"You should've said something a long time ago."

Rachael threw her hands in the air. "I tried to tell you when I first met you, and you thought I was nuts!"

"You thought I was someone sent by Ebony to trick you into

thinking I was me." He was up now, too, confused by his own state-ment. "At least that part makes sense now. You actually wrote a book about the academy, and everyone in it, and now you're meeting the characters you wrote about?"

"Yes. Welcome to my crazy, insane, improbable, yet very real world." She ran both hands through her hair. "You know what, I'm gonna go. This is all... impossible. Maybe I should've never come here."

"Maybe you should've never written yourself into our world anyway."

"You're right. Believe me, every day I think about what I'd be doing if I hadn't." She took a few steps toward the door but stopped and spun around to face him. "But then... it was worth it to meet you. And everyone else. I don't blame you for hating me, Graham. But I am sorry."

He stared at her for a few moments, his eyes saying everything. Rachael turned the knob and pulled the door open, wishing she could go back five minutes in time and kiss him before she told him the truth. Now, she'd probably lost her chance. Forever.

11

____

ARE WE DATING??

Rachael

A FEW WEEKS PASSED, and Rachael didn't see or hear from Graham at all. Jared said he was going on a lot of recruiting trips because they needed a larger fall class to make up for the shortage from the summer. He also said they were going on a lot of hunts, trying to figure out what was going on with Sasha, but they couldn't get a handle on her.

Neither could Rachael. Taking Jared's advice to heart, she tried writing a new chapter of her story. In this one, Jared was able to locate the book that Chell had used to lock Sasha away and recast the spell. It hadn't worked, though. She'd even taken Jared to the library and asked him to look around, knowing exactly where she'd had it placed in the book. Not only was it not there, he didn't find it anywhere.

Finally, one evening, Rachael sat down to write, thinking maybe the only way that she could get Sasha back in her prison was to resurrect Chell and let her do it. She wrote a detailed chapter about how she, Rachael, the new girl, drove to the cemetery in the middle of the night and commanded that Chell rise from her grave. In the book, the vampire hunter had pushed through the coffin and crawled out like she'd just been sleeping. As soon as she was done writing, Rachael left.

It was a hot evening, and she didn't like the idea of going out to a cemetery by herself in the middle of the night. But the only way to test her theory was to just do it. So she did. It took her a while to find Pleasant Grove because she got lost in the dark and turned the wrong way, but eventually, she found it.

The cemetery did seem peaceful. The moon was full, which might've freaked her out if it hadn't given the countryside so much more light than it would've otherwise had with no moon at all. She stumbled on some loose ground but found her way to Chell's grave.

There were fresh flowers on it. She had to assume those had come from Graham or Sammi. He hadn't said anything to Sammi about her revelation, or at least she assumed he must not have since Sammi hadn't tried to kill her. The trainer hadn't been any nicer, either, but at least there was no murder involved, which made Rachael assume Graham was doing her the decency of keeping her admission to himself.

Taking a deep breath, Rachael studied the grave. If this actually worked as it had in the book, the creepiest thing she'd ever seen in her life was about to happen. That was saying something since she'd seen Frank Merek the vampire meet his untimely death at the hands of the team of vampire hunters. Nevertheless, Rachael had to swallow her fear and just do it.

"Okay. Here goes." She inhaled deeply a few more times. "Chell Knight, I command you, through the collective powers of this realm and any others, to cast yourself forth out of this grave, and live again. As I, Rachael Barnes, the scribe have written, so must it be done!" She raised her arms and flourished them over the grave, like she had some sort of magic that would make it happen.

Nothing happened. The ground didn't shake. It didn't move. Certainly, no formerly dead now re-animated hand sprang forth from the earth. Rachael waited a good long while before she tried casting the spell again. "Seriously?" she said when all she heard was the hoot of an owl. "You've got to be shitting me. Yeah, nice theory Jared. But it's bullshit. This whole world is bullshit!" she screamed at the top of her lungs. The owl flew off, and she realized she'd just made Pleasant Grove fairly unpleasant.

"You really thought that would work?"

The voice behind her made her jump until she realized without turning around that it was Graham. "What are you doing here?"

"I saw you leave. Wondered where the hell you were going at 2:00 in the morning."

She turned around now, saw his car further down the road. "Why did you sneak up on me?"

"I wasn't trying to, but you were pretty focused."

"Well, raising the dead takes an enormous amount of concentration. Apparently, more than I have."

"Or powers that you don't have. Rachael, I know Jared thinks he's right about a lot of things--but they're just theories. I don't think you caused our two worlds to collide, and I don't think your dad's stuck in some in-between world."

"I see you've been talking to the prof."

"Yeah, well, after I talked to you, I wanted to see what the chances were you really did this, and that you could reverse it."

"And this whole time you've thought I didn't do it and that I can't fix it?"

"I still don't know if you did it or not, but I don't think it can be changed. Dead is dead. Unless it's undead, and then it can be dead--but it can't ever be alive."

She followed what he was saying. "Graham, I'm so sorry. I wanted to fix this for you, I really did."

"Rachael, you can't. You can't bring her back. You can't undo that. I appreciate the effort, but... Chell's gone. Forever."

"Okay, but what if there's another reality where she's not? And you can go there? Maybe there's a world where she's the accountant, and I'm the vampire hunter, and you could go there, and she could fall in love with you, and everything would be fixed."

"And I'd leave this world behind? No, Rachael, I don't want to do that. It wouldn't be my Chell, anyway. I don't want just any Chell. I want mine. And since I can't have her...." He turned and ran a hand through his hair. "It's just as much my fault she's gone as it is anyone else's."

"How do you figure?" Rachael asked, coming around so that he had to look at her.

"I was there that night. I didn't protect her."

"She was the strongest vampire hunter ever--how could you protect her?"

"She might've been stronger than me, but she was my fiancée. I should've made sure she was safe."

Rachael put a hand on his chest. "Stop it, Graham. It's not your fault. When I wrote the scene, I made sure there was no way you could get to her. You were fighting off three vampires, the rest of the team was occupied. It was an impossible situation for all of you."

"Then I should've called it off. I should've ordered them to drop back."

"And you did. It was just... too late. I wrote it that way on purpose, Graham. I didn't want you to save her--because... because I was jealous of her, okay?"

"What do you mean, Rach? She was an imaginary character in your world."

"Yep. But she had the perfect guy, a life I would've loved to have. I wanted to be Chell. That's why I named her that. Chell came from Rachael. But I wasn't her. I was sitting at home, my only friend a cat who is much more fond of you than she'll ever be of me. I wanted to show the world that Chell Knight wasn't so awesome after all, that she wasn't invincible. That someone could kill her--I could kill her. So I did. And it pissed off all of my readers because they loved her a hell of a lot more than they loved me. Everyone loved Chell--not me." It was her turn to spin around and walk away now. She made it all the way to her car and sat down on the hood before he caught up to her.

Graham sat down next to her. "I'm sorry, Rachael. I was way too hard on you before. I never stopped to think about it from your perspective. You had no idea that the person you were killing was a real person. She was just words on a screen to you."

"I should've told you the truth, though."

"You were right. I wouldn't have believed you. I didn't believe you when you tried to tell me I was from a book."

"True…" Rachael shook her head, wishing she would've never left the dorm. She shouldn't have let Jared convince her this might work.

Graham's arm came around her, and he pulled her closer so that her head was against his shoulder. It wasn't the same as it had been before all of this, though. It was more like he was hugging a buddy than holding a woman he was interested in.

"So what happens now?" she asked.

He shrugged. "We get Sasha--the hard one. You finish your training. Hopefully, we'll have a spot on the team for you."

She looked up at him, wide-eyed. "You think you want me on your team? After all of this?"

"Hell, yeah. I've seen what your powers can do. You're amazing with coffee."

She laughed. "I've gotten a lot better since then."

"I'm sure you have. We need you on the team, Rachael. You're a fighter, and we love that about you."

"Thanks." She wasn't sure who 'we' was, but she was pretty sure it wasn't Sammi. If it was Graham, though, that's all that mattered. "Aren't you afraid things will be weird, though? Whether you like it or not, you're still part of this triangle."

"Yeah, I'm okay with it. As long as it's not a circle. I like Jared and all, but I think love is a strong word."

That really made her laugh. "It's not a circle. You and Jared get to stay friends--I hope. Meanwhile, he can do his best to charm me into thinking I have feelings for him, and you can do your best to ignore me while I chase you around and annoy the hell out of you."

"That's not gonna work for me, Rach."

He sounded so sober, it made her drop her head. "I was just joking."

He ran a hand through her hair. "I wasn't. I haven't seen you in over a week, and it's been driving me crazy. Not a difficult task, but still...."

The energy shifted around her, and she was suddenly aware that his arm wasn't around her like they were old buddies after all. "What are you saying, Graham?"

"I'm saying... I can't do anything about it right now. But I do like you, Rachael. A lot. And eventually, I will be able to do something about it. But for now... if you like Jared, I'm not going to come between the two of you. He's a great guy."

She looked into his lavender eyes, not sure what to say. So she muttered, "Okay."

A crooked grin took over his face. "Okay? What does that mean?"

"I don't know."

"Well, I guess that makes two of us." He bent over and kissed the top of her head and then headed toward his car. "You coming, or are you going to sit in this graveyard all night?"

"I'm coming." Rachael stood. A slight tremor seemed to shake the ground beneath her feet, but it wasn't like the last two times. She looked at Graham, her eyes bulging. "Did you feel that?"

"Feel what?"

"Never mind." Rachael shook her head and got in her car.

1 2

SOMETHING'S STRANGE

Rachael

"Maybe you just didn't write it the right way?" Jared suggested, staring over Rachael's shoulder as she reread what she'd written a few days ago about Chell coming out of her grave.

"How else could I have written it?" she asked, growing slightly annoyed. They were sitting in his apartment, something she'd only done a few times, sipping lattes while they brainstormed ideas for getting Chell back and rid of Sasha. She'd told him about her unsuccessful attempt, but this was the first time he was seeing it for himself.

She had not told him that Graham showed up or about the tremor. One of those two items she did plan to disclose. The other... not so much.

"I don't know. Maybe you didn't back up far enough. Or maybe there has to be some reason she can come back, other than just a magic spell."

Rachael raked her hand through her hair. "I think we're grasping at straws here, Jared. Nothing is working. Maybe I don't have the powers you think I do. Or maybe when I wrote myself into this world, I lost them."

He was shaking his head. "No, I know that you are who and what I think you are. We've just got to get it right so that it works."

Raising an eyebrow, Rachael studied him for a moment. He sounded a little frantic, and she didn't like seeing him this way. "I'll try writing something else," she said with a shrug. "How far back should I go? Should I rewrite the entire story from the beginning?" She wasn't even sure she could do that, not and keep it completely accurate.

"No, I don't think so. Maybe... just... before she died. Maybe if you wrote it so that she had some sort of resistance to death that she could call upon to make it seem like she was dead when she wasn't really...."

"I'll think about it and write something later."

"You're not going to do it now?"

"No." Rachael couldn't help but make a face at him. "I can't write with you watching me."

"Why not?"

Rolling her eyes, Rachael gave him a playful shove. "That's just not how I operate."

"All right. But do it tonight, please? I've gotta see if we can figure this out."

"I think you're more interested in finding out if your theory could be right than you are anything else."

Jared's eyes widened. "That was rude. I want Chell back." He moved closer to her. "I miss her--and I know that Graham misses her as well."

"And you think if Chell's back, he'll forget I exist."

He scooted even closer to her on the sofa. "Maybe."

Rachael had spent enough time with Jared recently to know what was coming next. His mouth was on hers within an instant, his tongue teasing and then pressing her to open, which she did. Making out with her professor was the sort of thing Rachael would've never done in college or before her whole world turned upside down, but now that she was Rachael Barnes, Vampire Hunter, the idea was just wrong enough to be right.

Jared was taking things to a new level, his hands exploring places they hadn't yet, and Rachael was letting him because it felt good to feel good. His fingertips grazed her rib cage, his thumbs slipping beneath the lace hem of her bra, when a knock on his door brought everything to a screeching halt.

Pulling away, Rachael said, "That was loud. You should probably get that."

His lips on her neck said otherwise. "They'll go away." Warm breath ignited her skin.

"Jared! Are you home? We've got a problem!"

"Damn it--it's like he knows you're here," Jared muttered at the sound of Graham's voice.

Any chance of ignoring the knock and continuing on was out of the question now. Rachael scooted away and fixed her shirt while Jared ran his hand through his hair and went to see what his friend wanted. He pulled the door open enough that Graham would see her sitting on the sofa behind him. She smiled and gave him a wave, as if nothing had been going down behind the barrier of wood.

"What's up?"

Graham looked at her and then at Jared and then back at her before he finally stammered, "Sasha. She's been spotted. If we move now, we might actually be able to catch her in the act."

"Sasha?" Jared echoed.

"I'm coming with you." Rachael was up, her laptop closed, as she moved to the door.

The two men exchanged glances before Graham said, "Uh, Rach, I don't think that's a good idea."

"No, Sasha is unbelievably dangerous," Jared agreed.

"Please, do you think I don't know that? Look, I'm not saying I'm ready to get into the fight with her, but if you're going to fight Sasha Thornsby, I want in on it. I need to see this bitch from hell for myself."

"You could get killed," Graham said, looking her right in the eye.

"You won't let that happen. Now, you don't have time to stand around and argue with me. Go, get ready and all that shit, and I'll meet you when and where?"

"No, and no," Graham said, shaking his head.

Rachael pushed past him. "I already know the where. The when just has to be soon."

"Rachael! You're not going!" Graham shouted after her.

"I agree with Graham! You're not going!" Jared added.

A smile broke over Rachael's face as she turned to look at them over her shoulder. "See you in a bit!" Even though she was no longer writing the plots, she had a feeling they wouldn't be able to stop her from going, not if she showed up ready.

The men continued to grumble for a second before she heard Jared say he'd be right there and his door shut.

Graham caught up to her in the hallway, tugging on her hand to spin her to face him. "Rach... you seriously shouldn't do this."

"I know how you feel, Graham, but I need to go. I promise, I'll stay out of the way."

"What if she comes looking for you?"

"How would she even know I exist?"

"I don't know, but you knew she existed before you met her. So...."

Rachael shook her head. She was almost to the exit of the staff dorm rooms. "Graham, it'll be fine. I appreciate the concern, but really, you know I need to be there. I need to see what we're up against if I'm going to figure out a way to stop her."

"What makes you think we won't get her tonight?"

She rolled her eyes. "I just know. I'll see you in a few. You're in a hurry, remember?"

Reluctantly, he let her go, and Rachael hurried off to her room, trying to hide her smile. She couldn't think about the danger at the moment, only the excitement of the hunt. Actually seeing Sasha Thornsby in person would be almost as extraordinary as seeing Graham had been--and just as hard to believe.

13

___

LOOKING FOR SASHA

Rachael

HOW RACHAEL HAD ACTUALLY ENDED up in one of the two SUVs headed to Baltimore to intercept Sasha was beyond her, but there she was, wedged in the back next to Marcy and Flint. The entire team had been called out for this, including the two other hunters she hadn't met but had seen a few times, Viv and Miguel. They were in the other vehicle, though. Luckily for her, both Graham and Jared were in this one, along with Sammi and Ty who were sitting in the seats directly in front of her.

"Why are you here this time?" Sammi asked when they were almost to Baltimore.

She saw Graham's eyes in the rearview mirror as he listened for her answer. "I, uh, may have valuable information about how to... stop Sasha."

Sammi snickered. "Yeah, sure you do. Like what?"

Rachael shrugged. "I don't know. But I'm sure I won't spill any coffee on you this time."

"Only because we don't have any." Sammi shook her head and

59

turned back around, muttering something about Jared bringing his new girlfriend.

He must not have heard her because he didn't say anything, and he didn't turn around. Rachael didn't say anything because she didn't want Sammi to beat the shit out of her. She wasn't Jared's girlfriend, though, even if he didn't always remember that.

"All right, our tip says she's in an old abandoned house on the outskirts of Sykesville. She's not alone, though. There are at least three, maybe four other vampires with her. All of them look pretty menacing. We need to be cautious and watch each other's backs," Graham was saying as he pulled to a stop down a dirt road from the farmhouse he'd just described.

"Are we all clear on assignments?" Jared asked.

"It's probably not a good idea for Flint and I to be climbing around on that roof," Marcy mentioned. "From here, it looks a little flimsy."

"We'll just have the new girl float you up there, and she can keep you from falling," Sammi snickered.

Rachael laughed, even though no one else did. "Good one."

Graham cleared his throat. "Rachael will be staying here," he said. "Alone. We are far enough from the scene she won't need a bodyguard this time. Rachael, you have your ear piece?" She nodded. "Good. If I say go, you drive this fucker like you stole it, got it? As soon as we're all out, you're moving up here."

"Okay." She swallowed hard. This was not what she had in mind when she forced her way into the vehicle. She'd come to see Sasha, to see if a face-to-face meeting would bring anything to life in her mind about how to stop her. From all the way back here, she wouldn't even be able to see. At least she'd have the app on her phone. Still… it wouldn't be the same.

"All right. The other vehicle came in from the other direction. They'll move in from the north. Viv, Miguel, Tripp, and three of the seniors–Pete, Liz, and Kent. They have a lot of experience, but they're green, so be careful and keep an eye on them. They've got instructions to hang back unless needed. This is going to get hairy if Sasha's actually there. I don't have to tell you."

"Why didn't we call in any locals?" Sammi asked.

"No time. Our tip came from a retired academy grad who goes four-wheeling out here sometimes in the evenings and on weekends. He was out this evening and saw her."

"I bet he wished that four-wheeler was souped up."

Graham snickered. "He didn't think she saw him. If she did, she won't be here. Anything else? No, all right. Let's go."

They all got out of the vehicle, and Rachael did, too, because she'd been instructed to move to the front. Her breaths were shorter than normal, as if her lungs were aware that there were a bunch of vampires in the area. Perhaps she should've stayed home.

"You have a weapon?" Jared asked, catching up with her as he came around the vehicle to the driver's side.

Rachael nodded. She had a gun and a stake. She hadn't had much practice with either. This was a stupid idea.

"All right. Be careful." He smiled at her, but he didn't kiss her since everyone else was standing around.

A few of the others said the same, though Sammi just glared at her. Rachael climbed in behind the wheel and fumbled with the seat. Graham's legs were about ten feet longer than hers.

"Hey, it's right here," he said, grabbing hold of a lever behind the seat and scooting her forward. Everyone else was moving on now, though Jared glanced over his shoulder a few times.

"Thanks," Rachael said. The seat moving forward had brought her closer to him.

"I think this was a really stupid mistake," he noted, his lavender eyes inches from her face.

"I know. And I'm starting to agree with you."

"Please, don't do anything idiotic… like try to follow us. Or get out of this vehicle and run if you see vampires coming toward you. This isn't a horror movie, but don't go down in the basement."

"This SUV has a basement?"

He chuckled. "You're too important to get eaten by vampires tonight, Rach."

"I don't think that's how it works." She winked at him, and his smile broadened.

"I've gotta go."

"Be careful."

"Yeah."

"Graham?" He still hadn't moved.

"Yeah?"

She leaned forward and quickly kissed his lips--just a fast, almost nonexistent brush, nothing but a puff of air and a mild fraction of a connection.

When she sat back and waited for him to admonish her, she realized his eyes had practically doubled in size. "Shit, Rach....Remind me to teach you how to kiss sometime."

A giggle escaped her lips as he pulled himself out of the vehicle and hurried to catch up to the others. His face was a little red, and she knew he was joking, but the idea of Graham teaching her how to kiss was a lot more pleasant than the idea that she'd just volunteered to put herself into harm's way by jumping into a vehicle headed toward a vampire farm.

Rachael watched them fade out of view, noticing that Graham turned back and looked at her a few times. Jared might have, too, but she wasn't watching him anymore....

14

THIS ISN'T RIGHT

Rachael

THE VAMPIRE-WATCHING app was open on her phone as the team moved into place around the old, abandoned farmhouse. Rachael's eyes were glued to it, and her breath was staggered as she considered what might potentially happen in the next few minutes. She just prayed the whole team stayed safe.

She'd seen a vampire before in the form of Frank Merek, her old boss, and a person she'd considered a friend. What would it be like to see Sasha's henchmen, a group she couldn't care less about, destroyed by her team? Would they swoop down out of the attic or slink up from the basement?

Then, there was Sasha herself. She was by far the most dangerous vampire alive. Rachael knew that to be a fact because she'd written her to be that way. Visions of what Sasha would look like in real life, with her long, red hair, and her golden eyes, made a shiver go down Rachael's spine. What in the world was she doing out here?

Outside of the vehicle, the wind picked up, drawing her eyes away from her phone, which was fine as the team members were just closing in on the house. They hadn't discovered any vampires yet. Leaves stirred up from the ditches on either side of the road, scratching along the side of the SUV and fluttering around in the air before tumbling back to the ground and then lifting off again. It was eerily quiet, other than the scritching sound and a lonesome night-bird off in the distance.

The moon was bright but no longer full as it had been when she was in the cemetery. It illuminated the ground and cast shadows from the trees that tangled and twisted into something that could've become something evil with the right imagination.

Rachael double checked that the doors were locked, her gun was in its holster, and the keys were in the ignition. She couldn't imagine driving away from here without her team, but she had her orders, and she knew she was the most vulnerable by far. Perhaps the reason they hadn't encountered the vampires yet was because they weren't there. But then… where had they gone?

She was watching from Tripp's perspective since he'd come in on the other side of the building. She wanted to be able to see Graham-- and Jared, but mostly Graham. It was a lot like watching a horror movie. Her breathing was labored as she waited for that moment when the music ramped up and the monster jumped out of the closet. Except there was no music to cue her, and if there was a closet, in this old place, the door probably wasn't attached.

When it finally did happen, Rachael jumped. Tripp and Sammi were approaching the back room when a door in the ground, which must've been an entrance to a cellar, came flying up and three vampires came bursting out of it. Rachael squealed as the vampire hunters opened fire, hitting two of them and knocking them to the ground, but the third was moving in on Tripp. If Ty hadn't come around the corner just then and shot the asshole, he probably would've knocked the other hunter to the ground.

These were big dudes--at least seven feet tall, with long arms and legs, their claws inches long. The bullets had knocked them down, but that wasn't enough to end them. The teammates worked together to do their best to keep them down on the ground so that others could come in and stake them.

Marcy and Flint were there now, joining in the fight. The monsters were doing their damnedest to get up, clawing and scratching. Sammi went flying across the room. She formed a fireball in her hand and sent it at the vampire knocking him back down as she scrambled to her feet.

"Careful! This entire house is kindling!" Tripp reminded her.

"Then take that fucker out!" Sammi shot back.

It looked like the team was starting to get the upper hand, so Rachael switched her view to Graham and the rest of the team. They were upstairs, clearing the rooms. It didn't look like there were any more vampires upstairs, which meant Sasha had to be downstairs.

Just as Graham was heading back down the stairs, satisfied that the upstairs was good, Rachael heard a creaking noise behind him. Graham turned, and a vampire came flying out of another discreet door, this one to the attic.

The beast, what looked to have once been a beautiful woman with long black hair, threw herself at him. Her chin was covered in dry, sticky blood, and her eyes bulged from her head as fangs protruded from her jaw.

He didn't have time to draw his gun or his stake, and she knocked him down the stairs. He only fell a few steps before he banged into whoever had been in front of him, and that hunter opened fire on the woman, knocking the bitch off him.

There was a huge scramble on the stairs as Graham attempted to recover and the other hunters tried to get up there to take this vampire out and see if there were any more hiding in the attic.

This woman was vicious, but she wasn't Sasha. The downstairs had been taken care of. Rachael heard that call come over the earpiece she wore, and they'd checked the basement, which was also clear. Eventually, Jared was able to run a stake through the vampire bitch's heart while two of the others held her down. Graham climbed over top of that tangle and headed for the attic, and again, Rachael held her breath because Sasha had to be up there.

Graham leapt up and pulled himself through the hanging door. The floor creaked as he hoisted his large frame through and yanked his weapon.

The space was dark, dusty, and rickety, but it wasn't big, and as Graham got to his feet, he could see there was no place to hide. Jared yelled up to him, "Need help?"

"I don't think so." Graham turned around and took a few steps in one direction and then another. "No, it's clear."

As Graham dropped back through to the second floor, the discussion quickly turned to 'where the hell was Sasha?'

Rachael listened, but outside the SUV, the wind picked up again, and the hair on the back of her neck stood on end. She looked in the rearview mirror, almost afraid of what she might see. It was clear-- there was nothing behind the SUV--nothing hiding in the trees or ditches.

Still... her gut was telling her something was wrong. Rachael turned the volume down on her earpiece so she could listen. The banging of her heart in her chest was almost as loud as her staggered breath, but other than that, just the leaves on the ground, the bird in the distance, a slight whistle of wind....

And a scratching sound on the roof of the SUV.

15

WHAT'S THAT SOUND?

Rachael

THE SCRATCHING SOUND on the roof of the SUV intensified. Rachael held her breath, not sure what to do, but she had a feeling deep in her gut that this wasn't good.

Then, the scratching intensified, morphed into banging, and she thought she saw the ceiling above her give and then retract.

She wasn't sticking around to find out what happened next.

Dropping her phone, Rachael twisted the key and shifted into reverse as fast as she could, praying she was overreacting and some formerly unnoticed tree branch came into view.

Something came into view, but it wasn't a fucking tree branch.

Sasha Thornsby went flying off the top of the SUV, did a Peter Pan somersault off the hood of the vehicle, and landed on both feet in front of her, spinning around to face Rachael, amber eyes wide, fangs bared.

"Holy fucking motherfucking shit!" Rachael screamed, knowing she was about to go off into the ditch on the side of the road. She hadn't been looking behind her at all. If she got stuck, she was dead.

But then, it probably didn't matter anyway since Sasha was running after her now, keeping pace, speeding up, about to catch her.

In her turned-down earpiece, Rachael heard Graham's panicked voice. "Rach? What's going on? Rachael?"

"I think I found your fucking vampire!" she screamed. Realizing she was not acting like a vampire hunter in the least, she tried to get her shit together, but this was not exactly what she had in mind when she thought it would be interesting to see Sasha Thornsby. She'd meant from a distance--with people armed with weapons they actually knew how to use between her and the psychopathic undead demon witch flying at her windshield.

Sasha leapt forward, her red hair flying out behind her like a cape, and landed on the hood, digging her fingernails into the metal to keep from falling off as she looked Rachael directly in the eyes and smiled a gruesome, menacing smile.

Rachael felt the back passenger side tire go off into the ditch and slammed on the brake before she completely drove off the road. There was no fixing this by continuing to go in reverse. She couldn't steer it out, and she couldn't go any further back without losing more tires to the ditch.

Instead, she shifted into drive and hit the gas, hoping the SUV would dig itself out. Her tires flung dirt and rocks into the air, dust flying, but then, something caught, and she rocketed off into drive. Sasha slid, her face hitting the glass, but her smile didn't fade.

In her ear, she could hear Graham and Jared both screaming at her, wanting to know what was happening, where she was, etc. She couldn't talk, though. Sasha lifted her fist and slammed it into the windshield. The glass splintered and spiderwebbed but didn't break entirely. This wasn't going to work either.

Off in the distance, Rachael could see her teammates running toward her. They wouldn't be able to shoot from that distance, not if they didn't want to take the chance of hitting Rachael. As the vampire used her fingernail to dig a hole through the windshield and started picking pieces of glass off, her fingers getting slashed in the process, Rachael decided she was going to have to do something else.

She slammed on the brakes.

Once again, Sasha went flying off the car. This time, she wasn't so graceful. She landed on her ass in the middle of the road, skidded a few feet and then bounced up, ready to fight.

Rachael threw the car into park and drew her gun. If she could stay alive for another minute or so, her team would be there. They were closing in, and she'd actually driven Sasha most of the way to their location.

"Sasha Thornsby! You stupid bitch!" she heard Sammi screaming. "Come at me, fucker!"

Sasha hissed over her shoulder, but it was clear she was after Rachael. Why, the former accountant had no idea--unless she knew there was something "special" about Rachael as well.

Shooting from inside the SUV with the shattered windshield would likely just send glass into her eyes, so Rachael sprang out of the SUV, raising her weapon. "Go away, Sasha! I'm not even a real vampire hunter yet!"

"I know exactly who you are!" she practically purred. "Rachael Barnes." That creepy smile was back, and she was closing the distance between them.

Rachael fired, but Sasha was able to easily sidestep every bullet. She was less than ten feet away now. The team was still shouting taunts. Rachael glanced over and saw Graham was at least thirty feet ahead of everyone else. He wasn't going to make it in time, though.

With nothing else to protect herself, Rachael holstered her gun and raised both of her hands, palms facing Sasha. Narrowing her focus and concentrating with everything she had, she envisioned Sasha flying across the dirt road. But the vampire continued to come closer.

Now, she was laughing. "You think you have the power to toss me on my ass again?" she asked. Then, Sasha opened her mouth wider, grimaced, and hissed so loudly, Rachael thought she might've felt a little trickle down her leg.

"I can do this," she said to herself. Again, Sasha giggled. Just taunting her now, the vampire could've pounced and ripped her throat to bits. Instead she put up her own hands, her talons as long as a vultures.

"Now, you're pissing me off, bitch!" Rachael tried again, giving it everything she had. Why wasn't Graham close enough to toss her on her ass yet? Nothing happened.

Still laughing, Sasha said, "You don't have it in you!" Apparently, she was done with her teasing. Fangs bared, claws poised, the vampire launched at Rachael. A scream filled the night sky, and Rachael imagined it had to be her own as she braced for impact, certain Sasha would be knocking her on her ass in a second before she bit into her. At least it should be quick.

A flash of brilliant blue blinded her as she realized she wasn't moving--but Sasha was. The vampire went flying up into the air and traveled at least a football field's length in a matter of seconds before she came down on the road, hard on her back.

Rachael stared after her, shocked, then realized her hands were warm--the blue light had come from her. She'd done that. "Holy shit," she muttered, shaking her hands to make it stop.

"Are you okay?" Graham asked, wrapping his arms around her. Behind him, he saw the rest of the team redirecting their charge to close in on Sasha, but the vampire was up now. She wouldn't be easy to catch, especially since she could jump long distances that made it look like she was flying.

"I'm fine," she said. She almost asked him where Jared was but then she saw him. He hadn't gone with the others after Sasha. He was behind Graham, making sure Rachael wasn't hurt.

"Thank God." He kissed the top of her head and then let her go.

Jared was there in an instant. "You're sure you're fine?"

"Yes. I'm fine. What about Sasha, though? Shouldn't we chase her?"

"You're not chasing anything," Graham said. "Besides, they lost her."

"How do you know?" Rachael asked him. She couldn't see any of them now that they'd disappeared behind the tree line.

"Is your ear piece even working?" Jared asked her.

"Oh, I turned it down. I thought I heard some scratching on top of the car."

"Good call." He shook his head at her. "Car's a little scratched up now, for sure." He still hadn't completely let go of her, one arm still looped over her shoulders.

"Did you know you could do that?" Graham asked her, gesturing at her hands.

Rachael shook her head. "No, not until I did it."

"Thank God you could or else you'd be roadkill about now," Jared said, shaking his head.

"You don't have to tell me." Rachael's heart was still beating out of her chest, but she wasn't scared anymore. It was an adrenaline rush, the best kind, the kind you get when you kick a vampire's ass. Sasha might know exactly who she was, but Rachael didn't. She was interested in finding out, though. This new Rachael Barnes was pretty damn exciting.

16

ESCAPING SASHA

Rachael

DRIVING the SUV with the broken windshield back to campus wasn't really an option, nor was squeezing everyone into the one SUV that wasn't damaged, so part of the team stayed behind, waiting for another staff member from Silverwood to come and get them.

Graham insisted that Rachael leave with the first team, and he was with her because she wouldn't budge unless he came. As much as he wanted to stay there and make sure the rest of the team got home safely, Graham gave in and found himself sitting next to her in the third row of seats in the SUV. Tripp was driving, and Jared had said he'd stay behind and wait for the second vehicle. Rachael didn't miss the wounded look in his eyes, but it couldn't be helped at the moment. She was coming down from the high of using her powers against Sasha and needed to be with the person she trusted most. At the moment, that was Graham.

Sammi had stayed behind, too, which Rachael was happy about. The last thing she needed at the moment was more criticism from Chell's sister, although, she had to admit Sammi had backed off with the glares after Sasha had gone flying down the road. Even the sassy little trainer seemed impressed with Rachael's sudden abilities.

Graham's hands were in his lap, but his knee was next to hers, and she had a feeling he'd be holding her hand if Marcy wasn't on his other side. Every once in a while, he'd whisper a question to her. "Are you okay?" "Are you doing all right?" "Your hands don't hurt, do they?"

Rachael assured him that she was fine, though the more she thought about what had happened with Sasha, the more freaked out she became--followed by exhilaration--and then some sort of overly-emotional tears came to her eyes. She assumed it was all a result of adrenaline and shock and just kept taking deep breaths, focusing on Graham's leg against hers.

They pulled into the garage, and Tripp turned around so that he was looking at Graham. "Are we going to talk about all of this tonight, or...."

"No, not tonight. Let's just wait and do it tomorrow. It'll be at least another half hour before the rest of the team gets back."

Everyone agreed they were happy to wait until the next day and headed toward the dorms. Several people were muttering about how close they'd been to getting Sasha. She'd just sort of disappeared in the trees, which wasn't surprising for Sasha. It had happened more than once.

Rachael was ready to get back to her room and go to sleep. It was so late, it was early. Her head was beginning to hurt, and she was worried about how Sasha knew who she was and what that would mean for her the next time she came face-to-face with the vampire.

And she was sure there would be a next time.

"Hey," Graham said, slowing to let the rest of the team go ahead of them. "That was the craziest thing I've ever seen--and I've seen a lot of crazy things."

"You're telling me," Rachael said, walking closer to him so that their arms brushed from time to time. "She knew who I was."

"What do you mean?"

"She'd called me by name, Graham. You didn't hear that?"

"No. We didn't have a camera on you since you weren't supposed to be involved, so all I would've been able to hear was whatever came across your earpiece, and turning it down so you can't hear turns down what it picks up, too."

"Right." She knew all that. "Well, Sasha didn't just pick me because I was alone. She picked me because she wanted *me*."

Graham stopped and ran a hand through his hair. "Son of a bitch. Why didn't you tell me this before?"

"I don't know. I guess I thought you knew. But I also didn't necessarily want the entire team to know, if they didn't already."

"They don't," Graham assured her. He was still shaking his head, and by the look on his face, it was clear he was puzzled by what she was saying and what to do about it. "We'll need to talk about this at the meeting tomorrow."

Rachael didn't like the sound of that. She had hoped to keep her primary secret just between the three people who already knew, but if Graham told everyone else about Sasha, they'd probably start asking questions that would end up revealing the truth--that she had written about each of them before she'd met them.

Whether they wanted to go with her initial crazy explanation, that she'd somehow made them all real, or Jared's crazy explanation that she was somehow channeling another realm through a muse, or some other means, the fact of the matter was many of them would see her as being responsible for Chell's death, and that wouldn't go over well. It hadn't with Graham, and it certainly wouldn't with Sammi.

Seeing her consternation, Graham took her hand and turned her so that she was looking at him. "Let me think about it, see what I can do to figure out how we can explain it to them in a way that lets them help us decide how to precede and try to find out how she could know who you are without telling them too much."

"I don't think that's possible, Graham." She placed her hand on his chest, beneath his jacket. They were only about halfway to the dorm building, and there were windows looking out over them. Anyone with a room on this side of the building could potentially be watching them, though Rachael doubted anyone would be up at the moment.

Still, it could potentially be a problem for Graham if anyone did see and wanted to call him out on being too close to her when he should've still been thinking about Chell.

His mind was on Rachael right now, though. She could see it in his eyes, the way he looked at her mouth and then back at her eyes several times before he said, "I'll think of something." He ran his hand through her hair, brushing it away from her face.

She wanted to believe him, but it would be a tall order. She might just have to face the music with Sammi, the same way she had with him. He'd been so angry at her, but he'd gotten over it, or so it seemed.

His thumb caressed her cheek. "Rachael, when I realized what Sasha was doing, where she was, and that you were all alone in that SUV, that was the most terrified I've ever been in my whole life. Ever."

Her eyebrows raced. That would include when he knew Chell was in trouble the night she died. Of course, he likely expected her to be able to protect herself. Still, Rachael could see in his eyes that he meant what he was saying. Obviously, he cared a lot about her. "At least now we know I have a weapon I can use against her."

"Assuming it works when it's supposed to," he added. "I don't want you to go with us again until we're sure you're fully trained. That scared the hell out of me. I never should've let you come in the first place. I don't know how you managed to weasel your way into that vehicle."

Rachael smirked at him. "Neither do I."

"Listen, I don't want you to worry about Sammi or anyone else. I don't know how all of this happened, but I do know you well enough to understand now that there's no way you would've intentionally killed anyone, especially not someone I loved. I'm sorry I got so upset at you."

"I don't blame you. I wouldn't have blamed you if you never spoke to me again."

"I wasn't planning on it, but damn it, Rachael, I think I'm addicted to you." He was inching closer to her, and she was drawn to him like a moth careening into an inferno.

"If you're expecting me to convince you that you should do some-thing about that, I'm sorry to disappoint you, but I'm kind of okay with it."

He grinned at her, his lips hovering near hers now. "I am a horrible person, but I'm going to kiss you anyway."

"You're a wonderful person," she corrected, but that was all she could get out before his lips were on hers, and Rachael felt herself lifting off the ground, her mind floating away as the feel of his warm lips encompassed hers, the taste of him searing her tongue with a heat that she knew would burn for the ages.

Headlights flashed across them, and Rachael backed away, real-izing it was the other SUV. "We should go," she said, praying that no one in the other vehicle had seen them. In her stomach, she had a sinking feeling that someone had seen them, and with her luck, it would either be Sammi, Jared, or both.

Graham rushed her inside, and they both headed upstairs, but he had her hand, and it felt as natural as breathing.

When they got to the top of the stairs, she had to let go of his hand to head to her dorm room, while he would go the other way. "I can walk you home," he said.

"I think you'd better not. We've already got enough potential witnesses."

"All right, Rach. I'll see you later."

"'Kay, bye." She desperately wanted to lean in and kiss him again but didn't. Too much of a wonderful thing all at once could lead to something worse than addiction. It could lead to obsession, and she knew she needed to damper herself, or she'd end up completely obsessed with Graham.

17

ANGRY TEAM

Rachael

"What the hell was Rachael even doing there in the first place?" Sammi demanded, sitting across the table from Rachael again at the conference table in the staff lounge the next day.

"It's complicated," Graham replied, his tone calm and laid back, which Rachael assumed was part of his attempt to nonchalantly bring up the fact that Rachael had more of a connection to all of this than they knew. There was no reason to get excited about it, if he could avoid it, she reasoned.

"Uncomplicate it." Sammi wasn't giving up.

With a deep breath, Graham said, "You saw the power that Rachael has last night, right? Jared and I have been aware that there are certain qualities she has that we haven't been able to understand, despite our best research and inquiry. We thought taking her along might be the best way to ensure we reached Sasha."

"None of that makes any sense to me," Marcy said, much calmer than Sammi. "We've battled Sasha for years without Rachael there. Why would it help now?"

79

"Because.... Rachael is linked to Sasha in a way we don't quite understand," Jared explained. Rachael was sure that Graham and Jared had spoken about the meeting in private before it began. They seemed in sync, at least when it came to this. They were sitting on either side of her, and the steam coming from her leg nearest Graham was markedly different than the ice she felt rolling off Jared. She couldn't blame him for being upset that Graham had brought her home the night before, but that didn't make her hate it any less that he felt that way.

"In what way?" Flint asked.

"We don't know," Jared reiterated. "If we knew, it would answer a lot of questions."

Sammi was shaking her head. "Do you know?" she asked Rachael.

"No, not...." Graham kicked her shoe. "Not at all." She had been about to say "not really," but he was right, that would open a can of worms she'd regret putting on display at the moment.

"Do you have a suspicion or a clue?" Ty asked her, not unkindly, but it was clear he was still frustrated.

Rachael shook her head. "I don't know, unless it has something to do with my grandfather." Surely, that was safe to say.

"Wessley Barnes?" Sammi asked, and Rachael nodded. "Did he ever even battle Sasha?"

"Not that we know of," Jared replied. "But he wasn't part of the academy team for long. It's possible he encountered her elsewhere, and it wasn't reported."

"So... you took her thinking she could help, not realizing Sasha would be after her, but then Sasha did come after her, and she used that crazy rush of power to knock her on her ass." Tripp wasn't asking a question. He was just recounting everything for everyone.

"In a nutshell." Graham nodded, his hands folded on the table in front of him.

"And... now we just need to decide what to do about it?" Marcy asked.

"Yes. We don't want her going with us anymore until she finishes her training," Jared explained. "But we do need to figure out if it's

Chell's death that allowed Sasha to escape her prison or if somehow it's Rachael's arrival that triggered it."

"And… I want to fast-pace her through the program." Graham was looking at Marcy when he said that last part.

Rachael's eyebrows arched. She'd had no idea he was going to say that. She stayed quiet, though. It was fine with her, but she didn't want to seem so eager that she stirred things up with Sammi or anyone else.

Sammi was stirred. "What? Why? Because she can shoot light out of her hands at a great distance? So what?"

"Come on, Sammi. Even you have to admit that was pretty remarkable," Graham countered. "But that's not why. If there's a link between her and Sasha that will get us to the vampire queen faster, we need to use it. And this class is small enough that we should be able to streamline her learning to get her through faster. I'll talk to Dr. Mellow about it, but the rest of her current instructors are here. We'll keep her with the three of you until she's done with her program, if that's all right with you. We'll also see if Dr. Mellow wants to stay with her until she's done."

"Does Mellow know about that power?" Ty asked Rachael.

"No," she said definitively. She hadn't even known herself until it showed up.

"Keeping Rachael works for me," Marcy said, and Flint agreed. "You'll have to put in a lot more time than you have been, though, and be ready for us to kick your ass."

Rachael nodded, a smile creeping over her face, even though she knew Marcy wasn't kidding.

"I'll keep her as well," Jared said. His tone was melancholy, and Rachael knew he wished he wasn't talking about class.

She still needed to talk to Graham because she wasn't sure if that kiss the night before really meant something or if he would simply blame it on being afraid she'd be hurt by Sasha. By the way he was acting, it seemed Jared had either guessed that something had happened between them the night before when she picked Graham to go with her, or he'd seen the kiss when the SUV pulled in to park. Either way--she needed to talk to him, too.

"All right. If there's nothing else, we'll let you go. If we have another sighting, we'll have to be ready to go quick, so keep your phones close." Graham nodded at everyone, and they dispersed.

Rachael wasn't sure if she should ask to speak to Jared or Graham, but Jared was out the door before she could say a word to him, which broke her heart. He was such a sweet guy--the fact that she was hurting him made her want to cry.

Until Graham's hand was on her arm. "Can I talk to you for a minute?"

Her eyes turned to take in his lavender orbs. "Yeah."

"In private?"

Rachael looked around. They were the only ones there, but she knew that's not what he meant. "Of course."

"Thanks. I'll come to your room, if that's okay."

Thinking he was doing his best to avoid Jared, she nodded and stood. He gave her plenty of space as they walked out the door. Whether he was just being leery of wandering eyes or she should take that as a bad sign, she wasn't sure, but as Rachael headed to her room, her stomach was in knots. She'd only just started to think there was a chance the two of them could be together. Losing that hope now would be a blow worse than a vampire's bite.

18

HE'S INSIDE

Rachael

LEADING Graham inside of her dorm room was both a titillating and nerve-wracking experience. In her dreams, opening the door for him would involve him wrapping her in his strong arms and letting the door swing closed behind them as his mouth found hers, and the rest of the world faded away.

In reality, he stepped inside slowly and glanced around like he wasn't sure whether or not he could trust himself to be there. Once again, Rachael regretted having chosen Chell's old room. If she only knew then what she knew now….

"Are you all right?" she asked as the door swung closed. There was no kissing, no pressing of bodies, no colliding with the wall hard enough to jar picture frames, only Graham standing in the entrance with his hands on his hips, sweat beginning to bead up on his upper lip.

"Yeah, I'm fine."

"I'd offer you a beer, but it's not even 2:00 yet."

"A beer would be good."

With a shrug, Rachael went to the mini-fridge and pulled out two beers, giving him one and keeping one herself. No use making him drink alone.

"Thanks." Graham sat on the far end of the couch, and Rachael gave him some room, even though she didn't want to. He clearly had something to say to her that was making him nervous, and she was pretty sure she wasn't going to like it.

"What's up, Graham? Something tells me this isn't about Sasha."

He took a deep breath. "Not exactly. I just… wanted to talk to you about what happened last night."

Rachael's stomach rolled over and a sour taste filled her mouth. That wasn't the way a man brought up the fact that he'd passionately kissed a woman--unless he thought it was a mistake. "What about it?"

"Well… I didn't mean to kiss you."

"I know. You tripped and your tongue landed in my mouth." She said it playfully, but she was starting to get a little angry. He hadn't accidentally kissed her either.

He chuckled and took a drink of his beer. "No, I mean, obviously, I did mean to kiss you when I kissed you, but I hadn't planned on it happening until we got to a point last night where I thought you were about to be dead, and it scared the shit out of me."

"I seem to recall when that happened." Again, Rachael wasn't trying to be rude, she just wasn't sure what else to say.

"Right… so I kissed you. And… then the SUV showed up, and I'm pretty sure Jared must've seen it because he won't talk to me now. Nothing more than the bare minimum anyway. Were you guys… more than I thought you were?"

"That depends," Rachael said, adjusting on the couch uncomfortably. "What did you think we were?"

"I don't know. I know how he feels about you, that he really likes you a lot. But I didn't think… you felt the same way."

"I don't know how I feel about Jared," Rachael admitted. Realizing she was twirling her finger in her hair, she stopped and let it go. "I like him. It's been fun hanging out with him. But I've been pretty honest with him about how I feel about you. I think."

"You have been?"

"Yes."

"More honest than you've been with me?"

"Do you feel misled?"

A grin broke across his face. "No, but…. Never mind. It doesn't matter. I guess I'm just saying… if you and Jared were in a relationship, and I just butted into the middle of it, I'm sorry."

"We weren't. We aren't. You didn't." It was that simple.

"Did he think you were?"

"No. He might've hoped we were, but I don't think he was under the impression I'm his girlfriend or anything."

"Okay. Well, I can't blame him for being mad at me because he told me a few weeks ago that he had feelings for you, and I basically told him to go for it."

Rachael smirked at him. "How nice of you."

"Right. I didn't mean it then, though, and now I wish I hadn't said it. I fully intended to just wait until an appropriate amount of time had passed since Chell's passing and then reevaluate the situation. If you were single then, great. If not… by then, I figured I would've worked out how to deal with it."

"But now something's changed because Sasha almost killed me?"

"No, nothing's changed. I just realized life's too short to assume that I have a year to wait, that's all."

Clearing her throat, Rachael set her beer down on the coffee table and scooted a little closer to Graham. "So what are you saying, Graham?"

"I'm saying… I want to be with you. Now."

Rachael's eyebrows shot up. "But you're worried about Jared?"

"I feel awful about Jared."

Her head rocked of its own accord. She felt bad about Jared, too, but at the moment, she couldn't have picked Jared out of a line up. "He'll live."

Graham moved closer to her, and raising a hand, he brushed her cheek. Rachael's skin ignited under the heat of his fingertips. Placing her hand on his bicep, she scooted even closer to him until his arms were around her, his T-shirt wadded in her fist, and his lips came down hard on her mouth.

There was no use fighting it. Graham's presence made all rational thought flee from her mind as her emotions and instincts took over. His tongue tangled with hers, the taste of beer mixed with the sweetness she'd picked up the night before. His hand came around her hip, lifting her, and Rachael flung her leg over his so that he could move her onto his lap.

Straddling him, it was apparent he wanted her as much as she did him as she felt him stiffen beneath her. His hands were under her shirt, lighting a fire across her abdomen and up her rib cage as her fingers tangled in his hair and smoothed the hard surface of his chest. The deeper his kisses became, or the more he worked his tongue along her neck and collarbone, the more she found herself pressing into him, rocking slowly, unable to keep her body from responding to him.

Rachael wanted him so badly, she would've traded almost anything for him to lift her and carry her to the bedroom. She'd been dreaming of this moment since long before the real Graham had knocked on her door. Now, here she was, feeling his finger slide beneath her bra, as the other hand held her in place with his palm pressed to her hip.

But Graham didn't go further than the barrier of lace around the bottom of her bra. He'd barely touched the sensitive flesh which was longing to feel his heat when he pulled both hands away and then settled them gently on her arms, pulling his mouth away from hers. "Rach, we need to slow down."

"We do? Why?" She moved to find his lips again, but he was quicker.

Dodging her attempts to kiss him again, he said, "I don't want to do anything we're going to regret."

"I won't regret anything we do. Promise."

He chuckled at her and brushed her hair back behind her ear. "We have a lot of work to do, a long road ahead of us. Let's just... slow things down a little, okay?"

Realizing his mind was made up, Rachael unwedged her leg from between him and the armrest and bounced on her bottom next to him, feeling disappointed and defeated but also knowing he was right. "Fine."

"I'm sorry, babe. I really am. I didn't mean to take things even that far. I just… couldn't keep my hands off you anymore."

"Apparently, you remembered how."

"Rach, don't be mad." He grabbed ahold of her knee and gave it a good shake. "We'll get there. I just… haven't been with a lot of women anyway. Certainly no one since Chell."

"No, I know." She was being unreasonable. "I'm sorry, Graham. You're right."

"Hey, Rachael, you're really important to me, and I don't want to screw this up. So… just give me some time, okay?"

"Yeah, okay."

Graham got up, and Rachael followed him to the door. "I've gotta go see if Jared will talk to me."

"All right. Good luck." She had a feeling Jared would want to talk to her soon, too, and she wasn't looking forward to it.

Graham kissed her on the cheek and headed out the door, and even though it wasn't exactly what she wanted, Rachael would take it.

19

ARE WE STILL FRIENDS?

Graham

IT WASN'T a surprise to Graham that Jared wouldn't answer his phone when he called. Nor would the other hunter answer his texts. Graham went to his room and knocked vigorously as well but got no response. He was fairly certain Jared wasn't just ignoring him, though. There wasn't enough privacy in the dorm rooms for him to not be able to hear his friend (if he could even call him that any more) if he was there.

The only other place he could think of to look was in Jared's office, so he headed over there to see if the professor might be working on his classes.

His office door was closed, but Graham knew he was there. He knocked and heard Jared sigh. "Come on, Doc. We need to talk," he said, hoping he sounded sympathetic.

"No, we don't," Dr. McCall countered. "I've got nothing to say to you, and I can't trust a damn word that comes out of your mouth. So...."

"Please, Jared?" Graham countered. He hadn't tried the door yet but figured it was unlocked. Still, he didn't want to barge in. It was bad enough that he was standing outside the door begging to talk to him.

"Fine, Graham. Come on in, and let me hear it."

Graham stuck his head in first, making sure Jared was still sitting behind his desk. The last time he'd gotten into a fight with another hunter, it'd been Tripp, and it had been full of magical blasts and throwing objects at each other that had left them both mangled for a day or two. Luckily, both of them knew how to use the same powers that had messed the other one up to fix themselves a little faster than a normal human would've been able to. He just wanted to make sure Jared wasn't about to hit him with a bolt of lightning before he even got to say his piece.

"Have a seat, Graham," Jared said, setting aside a thick book he'd been perusing. "What is it that you have to say to me?"

Graham took a deep breath. He'd been wondering the same thing since last night. He took a seat but wished the chair wasn't quite so close to Jared. Now that he was in here, he wished he wasn't. "I just… I wanted to know if… if… if…."

"If what, Graham? If I want to murder you for telling me to go for it with Rachael only for you to change your mind a couple of weeks later and decide that you want her for yourself? Is that what you want to know?"

Running a hand down his face, Graham nodded. "Yeah, I guess so. More or less."

"Well, the answer is yes--yes I do. I want to murder you. Seriously, Graham! Why couldn't you just be honest with yourself, honest with me, back when we first talked about it? It's not like things have changed. You're just now able to admit that you like her."

"It's more than that, though, Jared. I can't quite explain it, but I don't just like her."

"Oh? You're in love with her all of a sudden? Two months after Chell's death, you're in love with someone else?"

Graham felt every muscle in his body tighten. "Can you… not bring Chell into this, please?"

"Why shouldn't I? It's not as if she has nothing to do with it."

"She doesn't."

"Of course, she does! She has everything to do with it! You were engaged to marry her!"

"You don't have to tell me that, Jared. I already know that."

"So--what you're telling me is that you just want to forget all that, forget about Chell, and jump in with Rachael? And I'm supposed to be okay with that, not because I have feelings for Rachael myself that you want me to just overlook, but you also want me to ignore the fact that the fiancé of my dead friend is ready to forget she ever existed?"

"I haven't forgotten that Chell existed, Jared. Don't put words in my mouth!" He could feel his face turning red now. Jared was purposely pushing his buttons, just to watch him explode, and he was doing his damnedest to avoid it, but something told him, if the professor didn't let up soon, he was going to lose it.

"I'm just saying, the excuses you gave me the other day for not pursuing a relationship with Rachael haven't changed."

"No, but my relationship with Rachael has changed."

"How so? You kissed her and suddenly realized that you can't live without her?" Jared said it with sarcasm laced through his voice, but Graham knew that first kiss had more to do with it than Jared could understand.

He didn't go there, though. "Listen, Jared, when I saw Rachael in trouble with Sasha, I realized that I couldn't possibly let anything happen to her ever, but certainly not before I had a chance to tell her how I feel. I can't explain it, Jared, but when she says that she created me for her, I can see why she feels that way. I feel the same way about her."

"You don't even know her."

"That's not true." Graham shook his head. "I know her. I know her well."

Jared gritted his teeth together. "I don't even know why we're having this conversation. The two of you are going to do whatever the hell you want to do anyway. Why are you even here? You want my blessing? I'm not giving it to you."

"I don't expect a blessing, Doc. I just want to know we can keep working together, that you're not gonna want to kill me every day for the rest of your life."

Running both hands through his hair and staring down at his desk, Jared said, "I can't promise you anything beyond this moment, Graham. I'm not going to kill you, but I sure the hell am not happy with you."

Realizing there was nothing else for either one of them to say, Graham stood. "I am sorry that I wasn't honest with you to begin with. I do value your friendship tremendously, even if it doesn't seem that way right now."

"Yeah, well, apparently not enough." Once again, Jared shook his head, and Graham decided with nothing more to say, he may as well go.

Somehow, he'd have to figure out a way to make this up to Jared, though he didn't even know if that was possible. He'd find a way, though. His friendship really was important to Graham--just not more important than Rachael was.

20

WE'RE A COUPLE—AREN'T WE?

Rachael

OVER A WEEK WENT BY, and Rachael wasn't able to speak to Jared alone. Even though she saw him in class, and he seemed like everything was fine, as far as anyone else could tell, she knew it wasn't. He'd sent her an email a few days after the hunt that said he'd be sending her extra lessons via email so she could accelerate her learning without having to come in for extra class time. She knew that was because he didn't want to be around her, and she felt terrible about the entire situation.

She'd been hoping she'd run into him in the cafeteria, but either he had stopped eating or was going at odd times. She tried varying her time, too, in order to catch him, but so far it hadn't worked.

Until one night, she was leaving the room, having just finished a quick pizza dinner with Rex and Jazz, when he came in just as she was about to walk out. In fact, he almost ran into her.

Immediately, he spun around like he was going to make a hasty exit without saying a word to her, but the other two newbies said hi to him, so he had to stop to greet Jazz and Rex, and then Rachael had her chance. "Dr. McCall, I have a question about my term paper. Do you have a minute?"

"I was just about to meet some friends for dinner," he said, suddenly deciding he needed to go into the cafe instead of running away from it.

"It'll only take a second. I'll see you guys back in the dorms," she added, to Rex and Jazz, so they would know they could go.

"See you," Jazz said with a smile that let Rachael know she was still under the impression something was going on between Rachael and Jared. She didn't know about Graham--no one did.

"Jared, you can't keep avoiding me," she said quietly as he debated whether or not to keep walking or listen to her.

"Why not?" he shrugged. "It's working so far."

"Is it? If those dark circles under your eyes are any indication, it's not working at all."

Letting out a loud sigh, he asked, "What do you want me to say, Rach?"

She looked around. A few people were starting to look at them now. "Can we step outside?"

Reluctantly, he went with her. Rachael went down to the end of the hall away from where the stairs were that came from the higher levels so there weren't as many people coming and going. He followed.

Running a hand through her hair, she said, "I don't expect you to say anything, Jared. I just wanted you to listen--while I say I'm sorry. The last thing I ever wanted was to hurt you."

He shook his head, and she wondered if he thought she'd done it on purpose. Finally, he said, "I know you didn't mean to."

"I never expected Graham to come around, not so soon, anyway."

"I know that, too."

"The thing is, I do like you. I like you a lot. And I had a lot of fun with you. I miss you, Jared."

"You see me in class," he countered.

Rachael rolled her eyes. "That's not the same. Professor McCall is not the guy I was hanging out with."

He was trying not to grin, but she could see it at the corners of his mouth. He knew he was different when he wasn't in class. "I can't just hang out with you, Rachael. Clearly, I have deep feelings for you, and you're in love with Graham. Granted, the only thing that's changed is now we know he feels the same way about you, but... it's different now."

The urge to ask if he just thought Graham loved her or he'd actually say that came to mind, but she resisted. That would be so incredibly rude. "It doesn't have to be different. I mean, we probably shouldn't be... kissing...." His eyes widened, and she wished she hadn't said that. "But we can still hang out."

"I'd rather not, if it's all the same to you. Not for a while. I definitely don't want to be there with just you and Graham."

She actually hadn't spent that much time in person with Graham since he'd admitted his feelings. He was still leery of other people finding out, and she was on board with that because once Sammi knew, her world would get a lot harder. "Come hang out with me and Jazz sometime--or Karma."

"They're my students, Rach."

"Uh... so am I. Duh." She rolled her eyes, and he actually laughed. "Tripp hangs out with the students all the time."

"Tripp is a recruiter, not a professor."

"Okay, then invite some of your cool professor friends over and me," she said with a shrug.

"As if there are any other cool professors."

That made her snicker, and he laughed, too. "Who were you having dinner with then?"

"No one. I am a liar."

Her face went straight. "I'm sorry you've been feeling like you need to avoid me. It's really sucked not being able to see you. I know it's weird, and I hate that it is, but I miss you, I really do."

A small smile came over his face. "I miss you, too. Not just the kissing, either. But you. I'll come around, Rach. Just give me some time."

"Okay." She decided that was enough for now. "Thanks for talking to me."

"Thanks for forcing me to." He opened his arms, and she stepped into them, giving him a friendly hug. It was strange since they'd done so much more before, but at least she had him back to some degree.

Rachael let him go, and he headed back toward the cafeteria. She took a few minutes to collect herself before heading upstairs. Her friends were meeting to practice their magic, and she wanted to go, even though she always held back when she was around them so they didn't feel bad about her abilities. It was just nice to hang out with them. It took her mind off other things--like Graham, and Jared, and Sammi--and Sasha. Always, in the back of her mind, she was thinking about the vampire she'd created. There had to be a way to stop her, and if anyone knew what it was, it was Rachael. Sasha must've known that, too, or else she wouldn't have come after her so hard.

She needed to figure it out soon, because the next time Sasha came after her, Rachael might not be so lucky.

2 1

EVERYONE HATES ME

Rachael

WORKOUTS WERE DEFINITELY MORE intense now that Rachael was trying to get through her program a lot more quickly than she had been before. Most of the time, she met with Marcy for a few hours after everyone else was done. But today, Marcy was busy. So she'd sent a substitute--Sammi.

"All right, Barnes. Now's the time to show me what you've got," the petite woman with the narrowed glare practically spat at her after Rachael was done with her warm ups. "First, we're going to do weight lifting, then, we're going to do cardio until you can impress me. Do you think you can impress me?"

She sounded like a drill sergeant, and Rachael was tempted to say, "Sir, yes, sir!" But instead she just sort of mumbled, "Yeah, I guess."

Taking a step closer so that her eyes were even with Rachael's mouth, Sammi said, "What did you say, Barnes?"

"I… uh…." She wasn't sure if she should repeat what she'd already said or say something else. "I said, yes. Yes, I can."

Sammi snickered. "I seriously doubt that. Come on. We're going to the bench press."

The bench press was not one of Rachael's favorites, but she had no choice but to comply. She knew Sammi could bench press almost three times her body weight, thanks to the supplements she'd been taking for years. At the moment, the most Rachael could handle was just slightly more than her own body weight--on a good day, when she wasn't afraid she was about to pee her pants from fear. She got into position, and Sammi loaded the bar up with enough weight that Rachael was sure she'd keel over the second she tried to lift it.

"All right, Barnes. Let's go."

"Are you going to spot me?" Rachael asked.

"No, I'm going to let you break your neck." Sammi rolled her eyes.

Rachael took that to mean she was going to spot her. She took a few deep breaths and did her best to lift the unbelievably heavy weight. She was able to get it up, but that was about it and had to set it back down.

"Seriously?" Sammi asked. "This is going to be a long three hours."

"You're telling me," Rachael mumbled, but then she realized what Sammi had said. "Wait--did you say three hours?"

"Try again, Barnes, and this time, put some effort into it!"

Even though Rachael knew she'd put all of the effort she had into it the last time, she tried again and got about the same result. Yep, it was going to be a long three hours.

After an hour and a half of lifting, Rachael was ready to crawl into a corner and die. Sammi was not ready to let her do that, though. "All right, Barnes, let's go back to the gym. I wanna see how fast you are."

Rachael's arms and legs were burning from lifting more weights than she had in her entire life. "Aren't you only supposed to do lifting or cardio on one day, not both?"

Sammi's eyes burned holes through her. "Are you wimping out on me, Barnes?"

"No, I'm not," Rachael replied, but she had a feeling she would be soon. Speed was not her thing, as anyone who was in her regular training group knew, but she wasn't about to just give up.

"All right. We're going to do some zippers. Does Marcy make you do those?"

Rachael nodded. She knew what a zipper was. Start at one end of the gym, touch the first line and come back, then run to the next closest line and back, all the way to the other end and back so that she'd touched every line on the gym floor.

"Great. As soon as you can give me a sub two minute zipper, we'll be done."

"What?" Rachael asked. "Sub two minute? Sammi, it takes me more like three minutes to do a zipper."

"Regular humans with no supplements can run an entire mile in four minutes, Barnes. Quit being a whiny baby and do it!"

Whiny baby was one of the nicer things Sammi had called her. Knowing that her best chance at running fast would be her first attempt, Rachael got into position and took off at Sammi's signal, running and stopping and running again as fast as she possibly could until her lungs were burning and her legs were on fire. When she finished, Sammi said, "Not bad. That was two minutes… and five seconds. Try again."

Rachael was doubled over sucking in air. She needed a minute.

"NOW Barnes! Let's go!"

Even though she knew she couldn't possibly run faster the second time when she had no oxygen in her lungs, Rachael tried again. The second time, she was much slower. Every time after that got worse and worse until, by her sixth trip, Rachael was pretty sure she was going to puke. If she did, she'd be sure to get as much as possible on Sammi's shoes.

"What's the matter, Barnes? Having trouble breathing?"

Rachael couldn't even answer.

"Here you are, supposed to be some great new find, some amazing recruit who can do anything, and you can't even stand up straight. I knew those assholes were wrong about you. There's nothing spectacular about you, Rachael. You're just like every other snot-nosed punk who comes through those doors, wanting to be some big, mean vampire hunter when you're really just a little sissy girl who can't even pick up the speed to save her ass!"

Rachael stood up and glared at Sammi. Why in the world had she made this woman so angry?

"Are you pissed at me?" Sammi asked, taking a step closer. "Do you want to punch me?"

Rachael didn't nod, but she sure the hell did.

"You think I'm wrong about you? Do you think you're special? Jared and Graham might think so, but they're thinking with something other than their brains, now aren't they?" She stepped even closer so that she was in Rachael's face again. "Your boyfriends can't save you now. If you want out of this, then you'd better run--fast!"

The temptation to blast Sammi across the room the same way she had Sasha made Rachael's fingers tingle, but she didn't do it. With her hands in fists, she went back to the line, and when Sammi told her to go, Rachael put everything she had into it. At first, she felt like her legs were burning and she could hardly move. She knew she was moving slowly again.

But then, about halfway through, something changed. She saw Sammi standing there with that look on her face, like a disappointed mother, and something deep within her kicked into another gear. Rachael picked up speed, and somehow, she felt her legs moving faster and aching less. It was as if her lungs could process air more thoroughly than they could before.

As she increased her speed, she noticed a different expression on Sammi's face. She wasn't glaring at her anymore. She wasn't smiling either, but she didn't look like she was watching the biggest disappointment in the history of the academy anymore. Instead, she looked sort of like she was slightly a tiny bit impressed.

When Rachael finished, she came to a stop beside Sammi, refusing to double over, refusing to suck in air, even though her lungs were tingling again.

Sammi looked at her for a minute and said, "Not bad. You can go."

Without another word, Sammi pivoted and headed toward the door.

Now, it was Rachael's turn to be pissed. "Wait! Sammi--what the hell?" she sprinted around and got in front of the other trainer. "Why the hell are you still being so mean to me? We talked about this. You know there's no reason for you to treat me that way, don't you?"

Sammi's eyes enlarged. "You think this is me being mean to you? Bitch, you ain't seen nothing if you think that's me being mean. That was me doing my job--training you."

"Bullshit!" Rachael spat. "I know you're mean to your students, but you've never made any of them do anything like that in class."

"That's because it would be a waste of time, Barnes. I wouldn't ask any of them to do that because they couldn't. I knew you could. So I made you do it."

"You didn't have anything to do with that! That was all me!" Rachael spat.

"Only because I brought it out of you!" Sammi countered. "Now, get the fuck out of my way before I show you what mean really looks like, bitch!"

Rachael wanted to say more, wanted to throw her across the room, but she didn't. She stepped aside and let Sammi go, still seething, wishing Sammi would just admit to the fact that she hated her.

Every cell in her body protested as Rachael picked up her water bottle, her bag, and a towel that was so drenched in sweat there was no point in wiping her brow again, and headed back to her dorm room. One of these days, she was going to challenge Sammi, and it was going to end in blows. She just hoped she was strong enough to defeat the tiny trainer when it came to that because the bitch deserved to be put in her place, once and for all.

22

A DATE

Rachael

THERE WEREN'T an overwhelming amount of restaurants in Waynesboro to choose from, but Rachael was content to sit across from Graham in the little Italian joint they'd picked out. It was their first official date, and she'd worn the nicest dress in her closet, a little black number with a plunging, though not obscene, neckline, and strappy heels. He was actually wearing a tie, too, which made him even sexier than normal for some reason Rachael couldn't quite articulate. She wasn't sure how Graham felt about putting out on the first date, but if it meant she'd have to buy dinner, she was cool with that.

"You know, it's called spaghetti and meatballs for a reason. If you're going to eat all of the meatballs by themselves, you should've just ordered meatballs with a side of spaghetti," he teased, watching her slice up another large ball of meat.

"Hey, I don't tell you how to eat your Alfredo, and you don't tell me how to eat my balls."

Graham happened to be taking a drink at that moment and almost spit wine all over her, which left Rachael with a satisfied smile. "So long as meatballs are the only variety of balls you're planning on eating, I guess I'm okay with that rule."

She giggled at him and continued to eat the way she always had, a little bite of meatball and then some spaghetti. The conversation was light for the most part, and she was just happy to be in his company. They hadn't spent too much time together since the hunt with Sasha over a month ago because Graham was leery of letting everyone know they had feelings for one another. He had the impression Sammi wouldn't be the only one who didn't like the idea of him seeing someone already. Rachael could respect that, so she'd given him some time and space and would continue to do so, even if not being with him was slowly killing her.

"How's training going?" he asked her when they were almost finished with their meal.

Rachael shrugged. "Not bad, when Marcy is there. But when she has a certain substitute fill in for her...." She couldn't help but roll her eyes. Sammi wasn't as hard on her now as she had been that first time, but she wasn't easy either.

"That's a tough situation," Graham said, shaking his head. The waitress brought the check, and he pulled his wallet out of his back pocket as he continued. "I'm not sure why Sammi decided she didn't like you right off the bat. She does seem to have come around a little bit."

"Yeah, but not enough," Rachael replied. "I wish she could at least just ignore me, but it seems like she'd rather seek me out and torture me than just leave me alone. And she doesn't even know about us, does she?" Rachael wasn't even sure if "us" was the right word since they hadn't talked about whether or not they were an actual couple or what the hell they were doing, but she figured he could interpret it however he wanted to.

"No, but I'm pretty sure some of them know we're eating dinner together tonight. Whether they'll tell her and how they'll choose to interpret it if they do, I'm not sure." The waitress came back for the payment, and he told her to keep the change. "What would you like to do now?"

"I don't know. What is there to do around here?"

"Not much. It's been a really long time since I took someone out on a date. Chell and I didn't exactly ever date."

"I know." She knew more than anyone else, besides possibly the two of them. She almost said that was her fault but didn't. If Jared's theory was right, then she wasn't actually responsible. But she'd gotten no closer to figuring out what had happened to bring the two worlds together since that day at his grandma's place, so she wasn't sure what to think about any of it at the moment.

"I do have an idea, but you might think it's a little weird…."

Rachael raised an eyebrow. "You hunt vampires for a living, babe. I'm pretty sure it can't get any weirder than that."

"Says the woman who may have brought two worlds together." He stood and offered her his hand, and she took it, following him out the door.

Graham drove her out into the country, but it wasn't back toward the academy building. She had no idea where they were going, but she didn't care either. He was holding her hand, and they were alone, and that's all that mattered.

He pulled off the main road and went down a meandering dirt lane for a few minutes before she saw a body of water flowing in the distance. Graham followed the lane to a spot near the bank where the stars were bright and the rolling hills behind the stream were lit by the moon, the stars, and a field of fireflies that twinkled even brighter than the heavens above them.

Getting out of the car, Graham went around to the hood, and Rachael followed. He climbed up and leaned back against the windshield, and she did the same, gazing up at the sky with the fireflies and the mountains before them. The entire scene was breathtaking. "I love it out here," he said quietly.

"I can see why. It's beautiful."

"Not as beautiful as you are." He raised and lowered his eyebrows at her, and she couldn't help but laugh, but then, they rolled toward each other, and Graham's lips were on hers, and nothing was funny anymore--it was just… perfect.

Rachael hadn't driven out to the middle of nowhere to fool around with a guy since high school, but once Graham's hands were on her, there was no stopping the longing she had for him. Her leg went over his hip, and he pulled her closer, the hem of her dress inching up higher with every movement, and she made no attempt to pull it down.

His lips ignited her neck as his hand tugged the fabric from the sleeve of her dress away so that he could access her shoulder, and Rachael let out a soft moan, silently begging him to trail those kisses lower. The fact that his phone was going crazy in his pocket was distracting, but she could live with the annoyance just to have his mouth on her.

Apparently, Graham couldn't. Mumbling a few curse words, he pulled back and yanked his phone out of his pocket. "Shit," he muttered, sitting up.

"What is it?" Rachael was up now, too, not yet righting her dress.

"Sasha. She's on the move again. Tripp's putting a team together. He wants me there."

"Tonight? Now?" Stupid questions--no, next Monday.... Still, she didn't want to see him go.

"Yeah, I'm sorry Rach. But I need to do this."

She took a deep breath. "I understand."

"I'll take you back home. We need to hurry or they'll leave without me."

"No problem." She managed a smile. She'd waited this long for him. She could wait a little longer.

Graham fired off a quick text to Tripp as they climbed in the car, and then he tore out of the serene dreamscape like a vampire out of hell.

After what had happened last time, Rachael knew it would do her no good to ask if she could go, even though she really wanted to. Despite nearly losing her life last time, there was just something about the hunt that got her blood tingling. But she bit her tongue. Graham had enough to think about without worrying about her. She didn't even bother to ask where Sasha was or who was going with him.

Once they were back at the academy, Graham stopped his car in the drive near the dorm building so she could get out. "I'm sorry, Rach. Do you want me to come by when I get done?"

"That would be great."

"It'll probably be pretty late."

"That's okay." She smiled at him but didn't kiss him in case others were watching. She thought he could come up with a reason why they were out together that didn't involve the word "date" but a kiss would throw that off. "Be careful."

"I always am." He returned the smile, and Rachael got out, but an uneasy feeling was beginning to bubble up in her stomach, and she didn't like the way it settled over her as if something awful was about to happen.

2 3

ALL ALONE

Rachael

DRESSED in a pair of black gym shorts and a gray shirt that came to her midriff, Rachael sat on her bed, thinking about what she should do now. Graham was off hunting Sasha, and he hadn't told her any information about the hunt, nor did he hook her up with the right tools so that she could watch on the app. He'd promised to come to her room after it was over, and while that was an alluring proposition, assuming he didn't just want to drink a beer and hangout, she was still unsettled and didn't know why.

It might be because she'd so badly wanted to go with the rest of the team. The idea that there were friends of hers out there under the blanket of night tracking down a dangerous vampire who had a vendetta out for Rachael, and she wasn't there, was irritating as hell. She understood why she wasn't there. She had almost gotten herself killed last time, after all. But it still stung, nevertheless.

That wasn't it, though. That wasn't the whole reason as to why she was feeling like her stomach was crawling with ants. There was more to it, she just couldn't put her finger on. At about 1:00 in the morning, she decided she'd poured enough nervous anxiety into one evening and turned the lamp on her nightstand off, thinking she should just try to go to sleep.

But sleep was fleeting. Graham had sent her a text a while ago that said they were having trouble finding Sasha again, that they'd found some of her clan, but not her. They were still looking though. It made Rachael nervous. Where had that crazy bitch gone?

Scrappy was lying next to her, curled up in a ball, and Rachael had just started to doze off when her cat made a screeching sound like a train whistle and flew off the bed, disappearing underneath the furniture.

Half asleep, Rachael sat up and said, "Scrappy? What's going on?" At first, she thought maybe Graham was there, and the cat was running to the door to greet him since she was so fond of him. But then, she glanced at her phone and saw she had a text from him that said they should be back in about an hour. It had only been sent thirty minutes ago, so there was no way he was home already.

Unable to rationalize what might be wrong with her silly cat at the moment, Rachael set her phone back on the nightstand and tried to go to sleep. She'd been in that sleepy state of mind when one's thoughts all jumble together and had been envisioning Graham coming into her room while she was still asleep to have his way with her. He'd just sat down on the bed next to her, leaned over to give her a sultry kiss, and then the cat screamed and ran away, waking Rachael up entirely.

"Crazy cat," Rachael muttered, trying to get the almost-dream back.

Then, she heard a familiar noise on the window, and her blood ran cold.

It wasn't exactly what she'd heard on the last hunt, but it was close. It sounded like the scratching of one long fingernail on glass--on her window.

Like any logical person, Rachael tried to rationalize what she might be hearing. "It's a tree branch," she thought to herself. "Just a tree branch."

But she knew how high up she was and how far away the closest tree branch was. No, it definitely wasn't a tree branch.

Still, it had to be something explainable. Maybe it was a bird. Or a bat. Or her imagination. Maybe it wasn't really anything at all. She closed her eyes and willed the sound to go away, and it seemed to stop. At first, there was just a pause, but then, after another scritch or two, it faded out altogether. Rachael closed her eyes, thinking Graham should be there in another ten minutes or so, and she just needed to relax.

Then she heard it again.

It was louder this time, more impatient, deeper, like whatever it was actually planned to cut through the glass. What's more, it was now directly behind her headboard, whereas before it had been further down the window.

Rachael knew what she had to do. She had to turn around and look out the window. She had to get up, pull back the curtain, and make sure there wasn't really anything there. That was the only way she was going to be able to get any sleep.

With a deep breath, Rachael pulled herself up to standing and turned to face the window. The scratching continued, still directly behind her bed. Her hand was trembling as she reached out to grab hold of the curtains. "It's all right, Rach," she said to herself, trying not to think of all the horrific images she might be about to reveal. Would she yank the curtain back to see Sasha hovering outside of her window, blood dripping down her chin, her red hair billowing out wildly? Maybe this was all a joke, and it was actually Sammi--on a really tall ladder, or with some kind of long pole. Whatever it was, she needed to see for herself.

Rachael took hold of the curtain and began to pull, but just like that, the noise stopped.

The night was clear. Thousands of stars twinkling out over the gardens and fields. Rachael took a deep breath and even laughed a little. She'd been acting so silly. Shaking her head at her own imagination, she let the curtain go.

And then she heard the sound again.

Only this time, it wasn't on the window.

It was coming from directly behind her.

Rachael knew she wasn't alone as every hair on the back of her neck stood on end, and her blood ran cold.

24

WHAT WAS THAT NOISE?

Rachael

Gooseflesh broke out all over Rachael's arms as the scratching sound she'd heard on the windows echoed through her room. It was coming from behind her now, and rather than sounding like finger-nails on glass, it sounded like the grinding of very sharp teeth.

She didn't want to turn around. It was inevitable she'd either have to do so or die with her back to the enemy. Something told her this particular villain didn't give two fucks about killing someone from behind. This was no spaghetti western.

Breathing--heavy breathing, in and out with a bit of a raspy crackle to it--took the place of the scratching. The curtains moved slightly, either from a shift in the air conditioning, or from the displaced air coming from the monster behind her, and Rachael caught a glimpse of a reflection in the window. Her blood ran cold at the sight.

It was like one of those awful horror movies she'd used to watch when she was younger, even though her mom warned her not to. Where the innocent, naive, stupid girl put herself in a position where the ax murderer could sneak up behind her, and then she sees him standing there in a mirror or a window similar to this one and begins to scream without turning to defend herself and then blood coats the reflective surface as she falls to the ground in a million jagged pieces.

Except this wasn't a movie. It was reality--a reality she'd brought upon herself when she unwittingly made vampires real. Now, she was going to watch her blood squirt across that window, staining the curtains, and probably spraying onto the bedspread she'd recently purchased, one she'd bought to entice Graham into her bed, one she'd hoped to finally use toward that end later that night, one that might just be wrapped around her in a little while to dispose of the body.

Unless she did something now.

Rachael wasn't going to die like that crumpled up blonde in the movies. If she was going down, she was going to put up a fight. The only weapons she had were her hands, but they'd served to be enough the last time she'd faced Sasha Thornsby. Maybe they would be tonight, too.

With her head held high, and her knee shaking so hard she thought she might pee her pants right then and there, Rachael turned around. "What the fuck are you doing in my room, Sasha?" she said with all of the intimidation she could muster.

Clearly, it wasn't enough as the vampire cackled, "Whatever the fuck I want."

"What do you want from me?" Rachael asked. "Didn't I knock you on your ass hard enough last time we did this dance?"

A grin split the vampire's flawless face. Her red hair billowed around her as if she was generating her own breeze. "I wasn't prepared for that then, Rachael Barnes, but I am now."

"I guess we'll see about that. My powers are a lot stronger now than they were last time, Sasha. I can probably knock you right through the wall."

She snickered. "I suppose we'll find out."

Rachael summoned her powers, and a soft blue glow filled both of her palms. Sasha stared at them for a moment, her eyebrows twitching. "Should I go ahead and get this over with?" Rachael asked.

"Shall I?" Sasha bared her fangs, and Rachael watched in horror as the two pointy spikes grew even longer, her lips pulling away to reveal a mouth full of pearly white nightmares. "You started this, Rachael Barnes. Don't forget that minor detail."

"I started this?" Rachael was almost so intrigued by the statement she forgot they were about to tangle. "What the hell are you talking about? You're the one who showed up at the hunt and tried to kill me."

"You're the one who made me into a monster!" Sasha screeched. She was loud enough there was no way Rachael's neighbors wouldn't hear, at least the ones who didn't sleep with electric fans on high. "I told you--I know exactly who you are! You're the orchestrator of all of this chaos! Your asshole friends might not have the power it takes to detect your origins, but I do. I've come to destroy the evil one who made me into a creature of the night! And I will not stop pursuing you until you are either dead or one of us!"

With that, Sasha came flying at her. Rachael raised her hands, narrowing her eyes as she braced for impact. Bolts of blue light illuminated the room as Rachael hit Sasha with everything she had. It was enough to slow her down, to freeze her mid-lunge for a few seconds. Rachael held her there, watching the vampire struggle to regain her momentum while fighting against being flung against the back wall, which is what Rachael had intended to do with her. Sasha was right--she was ready this time, at least enough to keep herself in the game. Rachael was going to have to do something else before her powers drained or the vampire overcame them. If she didn't figure something out soon, she'd end up just like the blonde in that movie, only this was reality, and dead was dead.

MAYBE HELP HAS ARRIVED

Rachael

"RACHAEL, ARE YOU OKAY?" Rex's sleepy voice called from the hallway. "I thought I heard something… weird."

Rachael stood in her room, hands up, doing her best to keep her powers charged as Sasha Thornsby, the most deadly vampire in the world, did her best to fight her way free so that she could end Rachael, or make a monster out of her.

The new vampire hunter had a choice to make. She could involve her friend, who was absolutely not prepared or powerful enough to help her and would probably get himself killed, or resolve herself to the fact that Sasha had nearly broken free from her grasp and was about to rip her throat out.

Rex was a good kid. He didn't deserve to die this way. As much as it would've been nice to have some help, she couldn't bring him into this. She also couldn't cut off her one lifeline. "I, uh… could you call Graham and see if he's around?" she asked, trying to keep her voice nonchalant. "Can you tell him I can't find my phone at the moment, but I'm having an issue I need his help with--right now." Sasha had worked her head free and was hissing at her.

"It's nothing I can help with?" Rex called.

"Nope. I need him. Or Jared. Or Tripp."

"Oh, I see." Rex's tone conveyed he thought she needed something else--something she actually didn't want from two-thirds of those people. As long as he was calling for backup, she didn't care. The only problem was, Sasha was starting to reanimate at a speed that would only leave Rachael a few more seconds to think of something to do to slow the vampire once she completely broke free, and unless Graham was already on his way up the stairs, he would be too late.

"He's not answering, Rach. Sorry. I could get Tony--if it's like, you know, an emergency."

Rachael looked at the vampire, now free from the top up, her arms clawing in Rachael's direction as she worked to bring her legs back to functioning. Tony also couldn't help her with this. "How about one of the upperclassmen?" she shouted. "Someone who's really good with their weapons? And tell them to bring a gun?"

"Who?" Rex asked. "Why a gun?"

"Just go, Rex! I don't care who!"

"Does it have to be a dude?" he called.

"Just go!"

Sasha was all but free now, and Rachael's powers were just holding her back. Her gun was across the room in the top drawer of her dresser, where she always kept it when she wasn't using it for practice. Maybe she could keep her hands up long enough to slow Sasha and somehow work it out of the drawer. Even a gun wouldn't stop Sasha, but she didn't have much of a choice.

Cautiously, Rachael took a few steps toward the drawer in question, doing her best to increase her powers. Sasha was actually closing the distance between them now, so Rachael hastily stepped away. She was in front of the dresser, but she'd need one hand to pull the drawer open to get the gun. With a deep breath, she brought her hand down and reached behind her.

It was enough for Sasha to overpower her. The vampire came

flying at her as Rachael reached into the drawer. She pulled the gun out just as the vampire collided into her, sending her careening into the dresser. The lip on the top surface bit into her lower back, and a few of the random items scattered across the top fell; something glass broke.

Rachael brought the gun around as claws bit into her neck. "Get off me, bitch!" she screamed, pushing against Sasha's chest with her forearm. The creature's breath smelled like death on a hot plate, pungent and sizzling. The odor burned Rachael's lungs and made her push harder. Sasha slid back slightly, and Rachel raised the gun.

With an ugly chuckle, Sasha slapped the gun out of Rachael's hand, and standing only a foot from her, the vampire hissed, opening her mouth like she was a Pez dispenser. Rachael screamed and threw her hands up, praying there was enough power left to blast the vampire away. Body braced for the blow, she froze, immobilized, eyes closed tight.

"Rach, Rach? What's the matter?"

Rachael opened her eyes to see Graham standing next to her, his arms on her shoulders. "What's wrong? Were you having a nightmare?"

Rachael looked around the room. Everything was as it should be. Even the items on the dresser behind her were sitting up. Across the room, her gun lay protruding from beneath the couch. Her neck stung, but it wasn't bleeding. The window curtains were closed. There was no trace of Sasha anywhere.

Rex was at the door with some Upper Fall kid she'd seen a few times but didn't know the name of. He looked like he was ready for some action, but not of the vampire variety. She rolled her eyes and returned her attention to Graham, noticing that he must've forced his way into her room because the lock was hanging. "I... uh... she was here." Rachael stopped herself from saying who she was talking about in front of the other two students, but she knew Graham would know who she was referring to.

"What?" he asked, looking around like maybe he'd missed her. "Here?"

"Yes?"

"Rach… that's impossible." He ran a hand through his hair and went over to the door. "Thanks for your help, Rex, Mike. I think Rachael just had a nightmare, that's all."

"Are you sure? She seemed pretty lucid when she was talking to me," Rex pointed out, concern written all over his face.

"I'm pretty sure. Thanks." Graham closed the door, and since the lock was broken, he slid Rachael's heavy book bag in front of it with the toe of his boot before he came back over to her.

He didn't believe her. She could see it in his eyes. She knew what had happened, though. She hadn't been dreaming. She'd make him believe. But first, she just needed him. He wrapped his arms around her, and Rachael buried her head in his chest, thankful he'd arrived just when she'd needed him most.

26

HE DOESN'T BELIEVE ME

Rachael

"Take a sip of water," Graham insisted, handing Rachael a glass and then sitting down on the couch next to her. He brushed her hair back off her forehead. "Slow your breathing."

Rachael did as he instructed, but her heart was still pounding in her chest. "Graham, I know what you're thinking, but I'm telling you, she was here."

"I want to believe you, Rach, but I don't see any evidence of that. How did she get in?"

"I don't know. The door, I guess. I told you. I heard scratching on the glass. Scrappy went nuts. I got up to look out the window, and in the reflection in the glass, I saw Sasha standing behind me. I turned around, and she said I did this to her, I made her a monster, and she came after me. I shot my powers at her, and she was stuck for a few minutes. Rex heard the commotion and came to check on me, and I told him to call you, but he couldn't get you, so he went to get help from one of the upperclassmen."

"But Rex said all he heard was you. He said you sounded like you were in some sort of trouble, but he didn't hear Sasha's voice."

Putting her glass on the table, Rachael scrubbed her face with her hands. "I don't know why not. She's not very loud, but she was talking just as loudly as I was. You didn't see her out there, right? Just her minions?"

"We didn't see her," he conceded. "But that doesn't mean she was here."

"What about the surveillance cameras around the building? Maybe one of them picked her up."

He nodded. "Jared is checking them now. If she was here, she should show up on one of the cameras."

Rachael hated the way he kept saying "if," like she was crazy. "If she wasn't here, then what was I fighting?"

"I don't know, baby. Maybe it was just a bad dream. Maybe you were having a night terror. People have been known to drive their cars while they were asleep. It's possible."

Bending over with her head in her hands, Rachael tried to clear her mind. She knew she hadn't been asleep. "I don't think that's what happened, Graham, but I'm exhausted. I'm going to bed."

"Okay, yeah. I don't blame you. Are you okay, though? I mean… are you… scared?"

Rachael raised an eyebrow. "Why do you ask?" She was scared, but she wasn't sure she wanted to admit that.

"Well, I was just thinking… if you're scared that it might happen again… I could, you know, stay here. Or whatever."

"Or whatever?" she repeated, wondering what that might entail.

"Yeah, you know. Whatever." He shrugged again, and it made her giggle.

Rachael ran her hand along his jaw. "Do you want to stay… or whatever?"

He shrugged again, like a little kid. "If you want me to."

Scooting closer to him on the couch, Rachael put her hand on his thigh and continued to smooth his face with her palm. "If you wanna stay… that would be… nice."

"Yeah?" An eyebrow crooked over an intoxicating lavender orb. Rachael nodded, and Graham leaned in and devoured her mouth with his.

She hadn't been sure what he was getting at when he'd asked, if he truly just wanted to make sure she was safe or if he was still thinking about what she'd been thinking about before Sasha showed up, but as his hands circled her bare waist and his tongue pressed deeper into her mouth, it became quite evident what Graham had in mind.

He scooped her up, and Rachael wrapped her legs around his waist. His hands went to her bottom, and he carried her the few steps through the divide to her bed, dropping her and then climbing on top of her, offing his boots and tugging at his jacket as she scooted backward across the bed, dragging him with her. Once his shoes and socks were off, he climbed on top of the bed, and Rachael began to unbutton his shirt.

She wasn't wearing anything under the half-shirt she'd had on since she went to bed hours ago. When Grant realized that, he made a low guttural noise in the back of his throat. His thumb slid between her breasts and his palm trailed the bottom of it, setting her on fire. How many nights had she fallen asleep dreaming of this man touching her there, kissing, licking, sucking her there, and it was about to happen…. He was about to be hers in every way imaginable.

Rachael grabbed ahold of his perfect ass and pulled him closer, feeling his hardness against her inner thigh as his tongue worked its way down her neck and his thumb finally found the right place, bringing her to a peak immediately. She moaned loudly, praying he'd tug her shirt off over her head.

A loud banging on her door had Rachael jumping and Graham pulling away. "You've got to be shitting me," he muttered.

"Ignore it. They'll go away," Rachael whispered, trying to turn him back to face him.

"Graham? Are you still here?" Jared shouted, and Graham dropped his head down to her shoulder.

"I told him to let me know if he found anything."

"Why didn't you tell him to do that tomorrow?" Rachael asked.

"Because I'm a fucking idiot," he replied.

"Graham?"

"No, you're an almost-fucking idiot," she corrected.

With a groan that had nothing to do with the hardness in his pants, Graham got off her and went to answer the door.

2 7

INTERRUPTED

Rachael

JARED BURST in the door as if he had no idea what he was interrupting, though Rachael thought there was no way he could be that naive. "Okay, so I checked all of the cameras, and I didn't find anything," he said, pulling something up on an iPad he was carrying with him.

"Nothing at all?" Rachael asked, disappointed. Maybe she really had lost her mind this time.

"No, nothing on any of the exterior cameras, including the doors and windows on the first floor. None of the exterior doors register having been opened other than the times the camera shows people who live here coming in and/or going out."

"And none of the windows opened either?" Graham asked, folding his arms.

"Nothing registered. But… there is something." Jared was done digging on his iPad. "I decided to go up to the roof to see if there was anything up there that might give us some clues, and I did find this." He turned it around and showed it to them.

Rachael didn't see anything. She glanced at Graham, whose forehead confirmed he didn't see it either. He took the iPad from Jared and looked at it closely. "What is it?" he asked.

"Drops of blood," he said. "See? There are three of them. I found them near the vent pipe on the roof."

"You mean that tiny vent pipe a chihuahua puppy wouldn't fit down?" Graham asked.

"Yeah, that's the one."

"So… are you suggesting Sasha's like Santa Claus in the movies and can just fold herself up and slide down a pipe?"

"I don't know," Jared said with a shrug. "But it's possible."

"Is it possible?" Rachael asked, equally as confused. "I mean, I swear she was here, but wouldn't there be a better chance of the blood being from a maintenance worker or something?"

"It was fresh," Jared replied. "I swabbed it. We'll see if it matches yours."

"You have a sample of my blood on file?" Rachael was even more confused now.

"No, but I can get one."

Rachael held her head in her hands. "I don't know what to think about any of this. I don't have any scratch marks on me, even though she did scratch my neck. Where would she have gotten my blood?"

"Maybe she drew blood but you healed yourself. Your powers are so strong now, it's possible." Jared seemed pretty sure of himself, and Rachael wanted to believe him, but it all seemed so… weird.

"What about second story windows? Any of those open?" Graham asked.

"No," Jared said. "None at all."

"And there's no other strange openings that aren't monitored or anything?" Rachael asked.

Jared shook his head again.

"Okay. Rachael will come in and give you a few drops of blood tomorrow so we can see if she somehow bled on the roof." Graham looked as confused and exhausted as Rachael felt. "Thanks for your help, Jared."

"Sure. Are you going to spend the night here tonight so Rachael's not alone?" Jared tried to be nonchalant with his question, but it was evident he wasn't as cool as he was trying to be.

Graham nodded. "I was planning to, yes."

"Cool. Good idea. We wouldn't want anything else to happen, not even a bad dream."

"Exactly," Graham agreed.

"All right. I'll see you tomorrow then."

"Thanks, Jared." Rachael gave him a warm smile, glad he was working so hard to help her prove she hadn't lost her mind.

"Sure, Rach. Hopefully, we'll get to the bottom of this soon and make sure she can't get back in. You guys have a good night."

"You, too." Rachael gave him a little wave and watched as Graham walked him to the door, letting him out and then locking it behind him, as if that would stop Sasha if she decided to come back.

Rachael took a few steps and found herself enveloped by Graham's arms. "I feel so bad for him," she said into Graham's chest.

"I do, too," he admitted. He smoothed back her hair and just held her.

Rachael tried to stifle a yawn, but there was no holding it back. She really was exhausted, and all of the heat from earlier had gone out the door when Graham had opened it for Jared. "You wanna go to sleep?" Graham asked, reading her mind.

"Yeah," she admitted. "I'm sorry."

"Don't be. It's probably for the better right now anyway." He kissed her on the temple, and she decided he meant because of Chell. At least he was still planning on staying with her.

Rachael climbed back into bed, and Graham went into her bathroom for a while. He came back out in only his boxers, and as hot as he was Rachael could only keep her eyes open as slits. He slid into bed next to her, and she nestled against his chest, glad to have his arms around her even if they both had their clothes on.

28

BLOODY HELL

Rachael

"JUST A LITTLE POKE," Jared said as he stuck the needle in Rachael's finger. It didn't hurt, but watching the drops of blood form on her fingertip was unsettling for reasons Rachael couldn't quite wrap her mind around. All she could think about was the fact that Sasha wanted to suck every last drop of blood out of her body.

"All right. That's it," Jared assured her, pressing a cotton ball to her finger after he'd gotten the sample he needed.

"Thanks." Rachael took some deep breaths and tried to calm down while Jared did whatever he was doing with her blood sample. She wished Graham was there with her to help her feel better, but she'd decided not to let him come, even though he wanted to. She figured Jared should be as relaxed as possible when he was jabbing a sharp piece of metal into her flesh.

"It should take a couple of days to get that analyzed, but we'll know soon enough." He smiled and dropped down into his chair. They were in his office, but Rachael was sitting on the same side of the desk as him. "How are you?"

She wasn't sure how to answer that question. Waking up in Graham's arms had been heavenly, but nothing eventful had happened. She knew they'd jumped ahead a few chapters the night before, and if it hadn't been for Jared, they would've gone even further, possibly so far Graham might've fallen over a ledge and never made it back to her. She settled on, "I'm okay."

He didn't believe her. She could see it in his eyes, but when he said, "I believe you," she believed that. He wasn't talking about how she felt. He was talking about Sasha. "I don't know how she did it, but I do believe that Sasha was in your room last night--or at least some form of her was in there, and it was real enough for you to think she was there."

"It was her." Rachael was certain of that. "When she slashed my neck, it hurt. She pushed me against my dresser, and I swear some things broke. I can't explain it." She ran a hand through her hair. "But then, what else is new? I can't explain anything."

"I understand that. I've been trying my best to make head or tails out of all of this from the second I met you, but I can't figure it out either." He shook his head, the frustration evident in his eyes. "We'll get to the bottom of it, though, Rachael. I know we will."

"Yeah, but in the meantime, she's trying to kill me. I'm kind of uncomfortable with that."

He snickered. "I don't blame you. I'm not real happy about it either. We'll just have to make sure that she can't get to you."

"At least I know that my powers are strong enough to hold her off for a while."

"Unless the only reason she wasn't strong enough to get to you was because she was in some other state, sort of like a hologram or something."

"Is that even possible?"

"Again, I don't know. I'm just saying, I think she found a way to get in, but I don't know how. If it wasn't her in the flesh, maybe it was some other version of her."

Rachael's head was beginning to throb. She rubbed her temples.

"All right--I think this is enough mental gymnastics for one day. I'm gonna head to the gym. Marcy wants to hand me my ass."

Again, Jared thought that was funny. "All right. Thanks, Rach. I'll get back to you as soon as I have an answer."

She smiled at him and turned to go, wishing she could say something other than thank you in return. Jared was an awesome guy, and she really cared about him, but things certainly weren't like they were between them a few days before. "See ya."

Rachael walked down the hall to the gym, her bag in hand, hoping it was actually Marcy who was waiting for her and not Sammi because she knew that Sammi had to have caught on by now that something was going on between her and Graham. She wasn't stupid, after all, and everyone probably knew that Graham had slept in her room last night. Granted, some people might've thought he slept on the sofa just to make sure she was safe, but anyone who knew Graham well probably knew something was up between them.

She walked into the gym and at first she was happy that it was Marcy, but then she realized Marcy didn't look very happy either. "Is everything okay?" Rachael asked.

"Just fine," Marcy replied, but her grim expression didn't change. "I hope you're ready to run, Barnes, because I feel like today is going to be one of those days that either makes or breaks you."

"Well, considering a vampire tried to kill me in my own bedroom last night, I think I'm ready to prove my merit."

"I guess we'll see," Marcy said with a shrug. "Let's do some zippers."

With a groan, Rachael dropped her bag and put her toe on the line, ready to show Marcy she wasn't afraid of anything--not vampires, and not trainers who liked to make people run to show them they were superior. She wouldn't be broken today.

THIS HAS TO STOP

Rachael

RACHAEL MADE it back to her dorm before she collapsed, but only just barely. Marcy had run her legs off. Even pulling from deep down to clamp onto the power inside of her hadn't been enough in the end. Though, she hadn't fallen over while she was in the gym.

Lying on the floor by the door, Rachael tried to get her breathing back to normal and gather the strength to go take a shower, but she couldn't move at the moment. Scrappy came over and rubbed up against her face, purring.

Spitting out some fur that stuck to her sweaty lips, Rachael begged her to stop. "Come on, kitty. Give me a moment, won't you?"

Scrappy didn't voluntarily get off her face, so Rachael used the small amount of telekinetic power she'd regathered to move Scrappy a few inches away. That was enough to spook the cat and send her scurrying underneath the couch. "Serves you right," Rachael said.

The knock on her door was soft enough for her to know that it wasn't Graham or Jared, so she decided to ignore it. Jazz wouldn't be ignored, though. The door popped open, and her neighbor was already talking before she looked down. "You comin' to dinner? What the hell, Rach? You okay?"

"No, not really," she admitted, rolling slightly to look at Jazz. "Marcy kicked my ass. I'm just gonna lay here and die."

"Girl, I don't know what's gotten into you. Why you wanna fast track through this program anyhow? They're just gonna send you away faster."

"No, I'm staying."

"You don't know that," Jazz argued, shaking her head.

"That's what they tell me. I tend to believe it." At least Rachael had the strength to sit up now. She hadn't told Jazz much of anything, and all she'd said to Rex was that she had a bad dream that a burglar was in her room, but she didn't know why she hadn't wanted him to come in, as if it was all part of the dream. He hadn't quite bought it, she didn't think, but he also didn't ask any more questions.

"Well, just 'cause you're doin' the history professor don't mean you can stay indefinitely."

Now, Rachael was on her feet. "I'm not doin' Jared," she assured her friend. "I ain't doin' nobody." That was true--though just barely. She'd been close to doin' Graham, after all. If it weren't for Jared, she probably would have.

"Go, take a shower, and come to dinner with Rex, Karma, and me. It's been too long since you hung out with your actual classmates."

Rachael knew she was right. "Okay. But you might have to carry me. My legs are about to fall off."

"Get your shit together, girlfriend. You got ten minutes."

Jazz walked out, and Rachael figured she may as well take an hour because there was no way in hell she was going to make it downstairs in ten minutes.

Miraculously, halfway through her shower, she got some strength back and wasn't too late to dinner. She walked into the cafe to see the three friends sitting with Tony and Georgia. With a wave to them, she headed over to get some food and then carried it over. Jazz was right; she hadn't spent enough time with them lately. She was really enjoying the conversation and had almost forgotten a vampire was trying to kill her until a sharp hand on her shoulder had her spinning around in her chair, nearly tumbling to the floor.

Sammi was so pissed, she made the Marcy that kicked Rachael's ass early look pleasant. Glaring at her, Sammi said, "You've got a lot of nerve, bitch."

Rachael's eyes bulged. "Wh-what?"

"My sister has only been dead a couple of months, and you've already decided to claim everything that was hers, including her man. Don't think that we'll just stand by and let you get away with this. You'll be with Graham--over my dead body."

With that, Sammi let her go and took off toward the door, leaving every single set of eyes in the cafeteria staring at Rachael.

"What the hell was that?" Karma asked, her mouth agape after the question was out.

"That was Sammi," Rachael replied, rubbing her sore arm from where Sammi had dug her fingertips in. "She's mad."

"You don't say?" Georgia asked. "But why?"

"Oh, she thinks I'm fucking Graham."

"What are you talking about?" Tony asked, dropping his fork into the middle of his pasta and not even seeming to care that red sauce splattered his white shirt.

"Yeah. He spent the night in my room because I had a bad dream, and now everyone thinks it's their goddamn business."

They were all quiet for a moment, exchanging glances but no one speaking until Jazz asked, "Well, are you?"

"No," Rachael scoffed. Then, taking a bite of her pizza as if it was no big deal, she added, "Not yet, anyway."

3 0

MAKE THEM STOP!

Rachael

RACHAEL WAS PISSED. She was channeling all of her anger toward the rest of her team into her target practice. Ever since Graham had spent the night in her room, several members of the staff were treating her like she'd done something wrong--particularly the female members, including Marcy and Sammi, but not just them. Even Dr. Mellow wasn't so nice these days, and it was starting to get old.

Crossing over to the wooden target, Rachael pulled the two axes she'd just thrown out of the red and white bullseye. She'd been close to hitting the center, but she'd been slightly off. She'd keep practicing until she got it right. Earlier, she'd emptied a couple of clips into a black form on the target range. She'd then taken it down, written Sammi's name on it in blood red, and taken it home to hang on the wall in her room.

Now, she was pretending the target was her former friend and still trainer, Marcy, and she wasn't about to let off aiming for her center.

She took aim, drew her arm back, and let the first axe fly. It spun

137

head over tail through the air and landed in the center of the red circle with a resounding thunk.

"Damn. I wouldn't want to be on the other end of that ax," Graham said, crossing over to stand next to her as Rachael took aim with the second ax.

"Don't worry. You're not the one I'm pretending to aim at." She studied the target again and then let the second ax fly. It stuck right next to the other one.

She walked over to pull them both out, and Graham waited for her, his thumbs in his belt loops. He looked as hot as ever, but she'd been avoiding him the last few weeks, since the situation with Sasha coming to her room. Jared had confirmed it was Rachael's blood on the roof, but they had no idea how it had gotten there, and Graham still didn't believe her that Sasha was actually in her room.

Walking back over to him, Rachael took careful aim again and let the ax fly. The sound of it sinking into its target was satisfying in a way she couldn't put into words. "Is there something I can help you with?" she asked. They'd been talking on the phone for the most part, and he'd assured her time and again he was still as interested in her as ever, but he thought it best if they slow things down. She agreed but for different reasons. She knew he was worried about the rest of the team; she was worried about him. The last thing she needed was to convince herself they were going to be together only to discover he wasn't ready to move on from Chell after all.

"Listen, Rach, I'm really sorry about some of our teammates. I know they've been treating you unfairly. I just had a little chat with several of them, and I think they'll let up now."

"Why is that?" She let the second ax fly, and it struck the bullseye near the other one.

"Because… I told them to. I mentioned restructuring the team if they don't get their shit together and mind their own damn business."

She raised an eyebrow at him for a second before she went to retrieve her axes again. "And Sammi gave two shits?"

"She did when I threatened to take her off the active team."

"Why would you do that?" Rachael had her axes and was headed back.

"Because I'm putting you on."

She stopped, staring at him, not sure what to say. "Me? Now?"

He nodded. "You're ready."

Knowing questioning his judgment might talk him out of it, she didn't ask him if he was crazy, even though she was pretty sure he must be to have made that decision. "Dr. Overbranch approved it as well?"

"Dr. Overbranch is in charge of the school, Rach, not the team."

Tilting her head to the side, she studied him. "What?"

"Yeah. I run the team."

"Since when?"

"Since forever. That is… since my dad retired from doing it."

Puzzled, Rachael swallowed hard. "But that's not the way I wrote it."

"It isn't?"

"No. Dr. Overbranch approved everything that had to do with the team, too. I didn't realize you were leading the team."

"You hadn't noticed?"

She shrugged. "I have noticed you run the meetings, but I figured people just looked to you because you've been on the team the longest."

"But I haven't. You mean we've actually found something different between the world you wrote and the world we live in?"

"I guess so." She wasn't sure if that was a good thing or not, but she'd be interested to hear what Jared had to say about it. As soon as she finished throwing these axes a few more times.

"We're going out in three hours. Be ready."

She turned and looked at him as he walked away before she shouted, "I was born ready!"

He laughed and looked back at her, a twinkle in his eyes, and Rachael let her ax fly.

3 1

ANOTHER HUNT

Rachael

RACHAEL WAS RIDING SHOTGUN. There was no way in hell she was
going to ride in the back of the SUV with any of those people who
had been rude to her the last several weeks. Even though Graham had
told them she was part of the team now, some of them clearly didn't
want her there. So, since Jared was driving the other vehicle, she was
sitting up front with Graham, and if they didn't like it, they could
suck it.

The hunt they were headed toward had nothing to do with Sasha,
as far as they knew. Graham had filled them all in a few minutes
before they loaded up the vehicles. Apparently, there'd been a few
sightings of a pale, scraggly looking couple coming and going from an
older home in one of the historic neighborhoods of Baltimore. The
informants were fairly certain they had to be undead, but the team's
mission was to find out for sure, and if that was the case, to take them
down.

On the way to the location, the team was practically silent, only a
few whispers here and there. Rachael was about as uncomfortable as

she'd been in her entire life, but there was nothing she could do about it. A reassuring look from Graham from time to time was enough to keep her from jumping out of the vehicle--or turning and screaming at everyone to just be nice.

He pulled to a stop a few blocks down from the location. It wasn't that late as far as hunting times went, only a little past 11:00. Because the historic district was near downtown, there was a fair amount of traffic. They'd have to be quiet and try not to draw attention to themselves, which would be hard seeing as though there were a total of 10 of them, all wearing dark clothes and carrying weapons.

"We all know what we're doing?" Graham asked the people behind him.

No one answered aloud but the four in the back--Sammi, Marcy, Ty, and Flint--all nodded or otherwise acknowledged they knew the plan. Since it was basically the same every time they moved in on a house or other residential dwelling, there wasn't a whole lot to talk about. The only person who was basically clueless was Rachael. She wasn't about to admit that in front of the rest of them, though.

As they quietly got out of the vehicle, Graham waited and then hung toward the back. Rachael stayed with him. "Since this is your first official hunt, just stay with me, and try not to get involved unless you have to. It shouldn't be too much of a challenge, since there are only two of them."

"'Kay," Rachael said with a shrug. He had an awful lot of faith in his informants if he really thought there were only two vampires in there. But she wasn't about to argue.

She was carrying two handguns with silencers and had also strapped one of the axes she'd been practicing with onto her belt. She doubted she'd need any of that, but the ax looked cool, and she felt like a kickass vampire-slaying machine carrying two guns. She tried to keep her shoulders back and her head up, but all she really wanted to do was take Graham's hand and follow him around like a puppy dog--just this first time, of course.

The house looked like something out of *The 'Burbs* movie with

Tom Hanks. It was all falling in and derelict. It certainly stood out amongst the other immaculate, mansion-like homes all around it.

"This is what nightmares are made of," Graham muttered as he approached the home. Already, Rachael could see other team members on the roof. She hoped they didn't fall through.

"Are we going in the front door?" she asked him.

Graham stood surveying the home for a few more seconds before he nodded and said, "Always do."

It was difficult to be quiet on the porch. The old wood popped and bent under her weight, so she could only imagine the give it had under Graham's heavier frame. He approached the door and pulled open the screen with a squeal, froze, and then placed his hand on the doorknob.

When he turned, it opened. She knew it had more to do with his magical touch than the fact that whoever lived here had forgotten to fasten the door. He pushed the barrier open and slid inside, Rachael following, trying not to let the screen door make any noise behind her. It shrieked again, but it didn't slam.

The inside was nicer than the outside, though it still could've used some help. The supplements Rachael had been taking had enhanced her night vision capabilities, but she hadn't been on them long enough to have the same sort of skills the rest of the team had. So she concentrated on Graham's frame and carefully picked her way along a wood floor that had seen better days.

"I've got a body in the back bedroom up here," Sammi whispered into their earpieces.

Graham's face fell. One of the things Rachael loved about him was his tender heart. "Not a vamp, though?"

"Negative. Elderly woman. Probably in her eighties when she died. Bite marks on the neck. Gone… at least a week."

"Yuck," Rachael murmured, imagining the smell.

"Thanks, Sammi," Graham said. "We'll take care of her as soon as we find whatever did it to her."

"Attic's clear," Flint said. Rachael heard movement above her and wondered if that was the team on the second floor or the team in the attic.

"Back of the first floor is clear," Jared said.

"Tripp? What about the basement?" Graham wanted to know.

Tripp didn't answer right away, and since it seemed the only human resident of the home was dead, Graham picked up his pace, clearly looking for the interior entrance to the basement since Tripp and Miguel had gone in through a window.

Graham found the door that led downstairs under the stairs near the dining room table at the same time that Jared and Viv came into the dining room from the kitchen. The three of them exchanged glances that let them know exactly what was about to happen as Rachael stood there, trying to stay out of the way.

On a silent three-count, Graham pulled the door open, weapon in hand, pointing it into the blackness as Jared and Viv came in from opposite sides. The stairs were clear, but it was dark, only a few streams of moonlight illuminating an odd number of steps while dust and cobwebs settled from the disruption of having the door thrown open so furiously.

A silence settled over them that made the hair on Rachael's arms stand on end. Where were Tripp and Miguel? Why hadn't they reported? If they were in the middle of a shootout or a fight, that would be audible. So, what the hell was going on?

As quietly as possible, Graham started down the stairs, the boards creaking under his feet. Jared gestured for Rachael to follow Graham, which she did, then Viv, with Jared coming down last, leaving the door open behind him. Rachael didn't pull her gun because, at this point, she was more afraid of shooting one of her teammates than actually hitting a vampire. Besides, her hands were just as good a weapon as any bullet. She double checked that she had a wooden stake or two in the interior pockets of her jacket and was glad she hadn't forgotten the most important weapon of all.

The sound of Tripp's voice in her earpiece was welcome, until she realized what he was saying. In the lightest whisper she'd ever heard, he asked, "Is that you on the stairs Graham?"

"Affirmative," he whispered back.

"Be as quiet as possible," Tripp breathed.

"Why?" Graham asked.

"You'll see."

The answer was unsettling for a number of reasons, but when Graham reached the bottom of the stairs and stopped abruptly, Rachael rested her hand on his shoulder and peered out into the moonlit space.

Tripp and Miguel were standing in the middle of a large, unfinished basement, guns drawn, backs to each other--surrounded by at least a hundred open coffins, each one containing a sleeping vampire.

"Holy shit," Rachael mouthed.

"We're gonna need backup," Graham said.

Rachael didn't think the rest of the team members already in the house were going to be enough, but they'd have to do, because the vampires closest to the two hunters in the center of the room were already stirring, and as soon as they opened their eyes, all hell would break loose.

3 2

VAMPIRE HELL

Rachael

"WHAT DO WE DO?" Tripp asked, his mouth moving, but hardly enough sound transferring out of it to be audible over the earpieces. Rachael could see well enough in the dim light to know what he was saying.

"Aim carefully," Graham replied. "You two take the ones closest to you. Jared, clear the left. I'll clear the right. Rachael, stay here."

"Nope. I'll get the ones right in front of us," she said. Not that any of them would die without being stabbed with a stake, and they sure the hell didn't bring enough to go around. At this point, all they could do was take out as many as they could and then get the hell out of Dodge.

"How is this possible? Where did they all come from?" Jared whispered behind her.

"Don't know. No time to find out." Graham had a gun in each hand, and when the vampires closest to Tripp and Miguel suddenly sat up, alarming the rest of their kind, it was time to start shooting.

147

The chaos in front of her made it almost impossible to keep up. Rachael took aim at the vampires closest to her, firing for their heads since that was one way to make sure they were slowed, but she had to be careful not to hit her teammates who were standing behind them. Shot after silent shot filled the space. The only way to tell how quickly the vampires were being struck was through their reactions-- heads flying backward, bodies crumpling to the ground.

Rachael stayed on the stairs, trying to protect their exit but also because Graham had told her to stay back. As the rest of the team came flying down to help, she tried to stay out of the way. Most of the team stepped around her, but Sammi gave her a hard shove in the shoulder and shouted, "Out of the way, bitch. We have work to do."

Hitting the stair rail hard, Rachael rubbed her shoulder where it smarted from the blow. She wanted to accidentally aim at the trainer instead of the vampires, but she resisted the temptation.

The few seconds it took her to recover from the collision allowed the enemy to get slightly closer to her. Rachael fired off a few more rounds, but they were still coming. She realized her gun was not the most deadly weapon she had on her and shoved it back into its holster. As a pair of vampires closed in on her, Rachael raised her hands and concentrated on getting them to stop.

She did more than stop them. As the pulse of power left her hands and made contact with the two scraggly vampires, it was more than they could handle. The first vampire, an older man with blood dripping down his chin, had a pained look overcome his face before his entire head exploded into a thousand pieces, spewing flesh, blood, and bone everywhere. Two seconds later, the woman behind him blew her top as well.

Rachael looked at her hands, shocked. How in the world had she done that? Had she done that?

The rest of the team looked around in surprise as well, a few of them asking what the hell had just happened. Rachael didn't have too much time to think about it at the moment. Instead, she set her sights on the next two vampires nearest her and immediately made quick work of their heads, too.

"Holy shit!" Graham said, still fighting off the bloodsuckers while Rachael explored how much power she had and how long this new skill might last. As she continued to explode the heads off the vampires around her, the bodies of the fallen began to wiggle on the floor. They were doing their best to get up, despite the fact that they had no heads.

"Well, that's… insane," Jared said, kicking a vampire in the gut that had gotten too close to him.

"Someone start stabbing those fuckers while she blows their heads off," Tripp suggested.

"You volunteering?" Sammi asked, ramming her stake into the heart of an older woman with a limp.

"I would if I could," Tripp replied, taking down another vamp but turning to another one almost immediately.

Rachael was on her tenth or twelfth exploding head by now, but no one was free to kill the ones that were on the ground. One of the first she'd taken out was up, staggering around aimlessly with no head. "At least they can't bite us," she murmured. Nor could they figure out where the enemy was. With about forty more vampires coming at her teammates, Rachael closed her eyes and concentrated on the heads of the undead, praying this worked, and she didn't accidentally take out the hunters, too.

After about ten seconds, she heard the sound she'd been longing for and opened her eyes to see her teammates staring wide-eyed, blood and pieces of flesh dripping from their faces.

"I guess that handles that," Jared finally managed for all of them.

"I have no words," Graham replied.

Rachael had her stake out now, and no longer worried about exploding heads, she started stabbing bodies. The rest of her team joined in, though some of them were also busy wiping remnants of vampire brains from their faces and hair. She jabbed her stake into one heart after another, working her way through them as quickly as possible, putting her boot on a chest when necessary to hold the fucker down.

With the entire team working together, the last of the wiggling vampires was down before too long, leaving them all staring at each other.

"I have never heard of anything like that," Tripp finally said when it was over. "How the hell did you know you could do that?"

"I didn't," she admitted. "I didn't mean to at first, but after the first two blew, I decided to keep at it."

"This is a game changer," Graham commented, finally taking a second to wipe blood off his forehead.

"I don't think it works on stronger vampires, though," Rachael noted. "I doubt it would work on Sasha."

"Still...." He didn't say more. He didn't need to. "All right... easiest way to take care of this is a controlled burn."

The rest of the team agreed, and they went into action, preparing to burn the house to the ground but not any of the surrounding houses. Rachael had no idea how that would be done, so when Jared said he'd take her out to the van, she went with him, still trying to wrap her mind around what had just happened.

"You okay?" Jared asked her.

"I think so. How did I do that?"

"I don't know. But it sure was cool."

She agreed it had come in handy, but it made her wonder what else she could do. She followed him to the van and got in, taking some deep breaths. He got in the driver's side, and after a few minutes, he put his hand on top of hers. She let him. It seemed a little odd at first, but then it was comforting, and she started to wonder if maybe the situation with Jared wasn't over after all.

A few moments later, everyone was out of the house and heading back to the SUVs except for Graham. A minute later, the house went up in an enormous blaze, smoke billowing out the top, flames licking the windows. She watched, knowing he'd have to appear soon enough. It took longer than she'd hoped, but when she saw him walking across the yard, she let out a deep breath.

Jared started the vehicle, and Graham waved as he headed to the second one. In the distance, sirens sounded as fire trucks headed to the sight. With the size of the flames, there was no doubt there'd be nothing left of the house by the time they got there.

3 3

———

WAS THAT REAL?

Rachael

ARRIVING BACK AT THE GARAGE, Rachael took a deep breath and wondered what might happen next. Everyone was bound to want to ask her questions about what had happened, and Rachael had no answers. All she wanted to do was go take a shower and go to sleep-- possibly in Graham's arms.

The other SUV pulled in shortly after them, but Rachael didn't wait for him. Waiting for him meant waiting for a million questions from other people. She had no desire to answer any of them.

He caught up with her anyway. "Rach?" He took her gently by the arm and pulled her toward him, spinning her around as he did so.

"Yeah?" She looked into his lavender eyes and saw the plethora of questions there.

"Are you okay?"

"Yeah." That wasn't necessarily true, but there was no time to go over it all right now. Looking at him, feeling his touch, had her forgetting all about anything else. She just wanted his arms around

153

her. She didn't even care about the vampire parts both of them had all over their clothes.

He studied her for a second, and it was obvious he didn't believe her. "Okay. I'm going to go take a shower, and then I'll come over, if you want."

Rachael raised an eyebrow at him. "I have a shower."

Graham grinned at her, that easy, crooked grin that lit her on fire. "True. But then, I would only have my vampire goo covered clothes to put on."

"Who says you need clothes?" Her face was completely serious until he laughed, then she did, too.

"I will need clothes… eventually. I'll be over in a bit. All right?"

"All right." She let him go, and he was in such a rush to get into the dorm room, she didn't even try to stay with him. Instead, she stood outside for a few moments and took some deep breaths, trying to calm her racing pulse. It was the wrong thing to do.

"Hey! Barnes!" Sammi's voice cut through the calm and made her jump. Rachael turned around to see the trainer coming at her. She caught Jared's eyes as he walked past toward the building. She knew he would come and rescue her if she wanted him to, but she also thought Sammi had to be a little concerned that she could blow her head off if she wanted to.

Which ended up being the whole point of Sammi stopping her. "How did you know you could do that?"

"I didn't," Rachael admitted. "I just… imagined it happening. And it did."

"And when you blew them all up at the same time, how did you know you could do that without hurting any of us?"

"Well, I did it the same way I'd done it when it was just one or two. I just imagined all of the vampires exploding, none of the hunters."

"That seems like a risky game to play, Barnes."

"True. But… I had a feeling it wouldn't work against anyone with any level of power. Those vampires were all weak. There were just a lot of them. I'm sure I couldn't do it to Sasha or someone near her caliber."

Sammi wasn't done yet. Her arms were folded. Little pieces of vampire dotted her entire front and clung to her hair. "I'd appreciate it if you didn't take chances like that anymore. I'd just as soon keep my head from exploding, if you don't mind."

"Right. I'll keep that in mind. Sorry."

"You're probably right, though. Sasha's powerful. Trying to kill her that way probably wouldn't get you very far--as much as I'd love to see that bitch's head explode."

"Me, too," Rachael admitted. "I'm sure you'd like to see her gone even more than me."

"Damn straight. I don't know what her fixation is with you all of a sudden. Perhaps it's just because my sister is gone, and she can't get her vengeance on Chell now. She needed someone else. I don't know. But, yeah, I'd like to rip her fucking head off."

"Vengeance for Chell locking her in the cave?" Rachael clarified, not exactly sure what Sammi was getting at. She seemed to be hinting at something else.

Sammi's eyes were wide as she studied Rachael's face. "Uh, yeah, that and getting her turned in the first place."

Rachael arched an eyebrow. "What? Getting her turned? Into a vampire?"

"Yeah. I thought you were supposed to know all of this shit already for some reason. My sister and Sasha used to go to high school together. They were friends. Sasha blamed Chell for taking her to a party that had vampires their senior year. My sister knew there were vampires there, but Sasha didn't. One of them bit her. Sasha blamed Chell. That's why she focused on growing her power, so she could defeat my sister. Chell couldn't kill her because they'd been friends. She'd never forgive herself, so she locked her up instead. But some-how, when Chell died, Sasha got free. Now she's after you, and I don't know why."

Everything Sammi was saying was wrong--yet it was clear she believed it. "Wait--Sasha and Chell couldn't have gone to school together. Sasha's been a vampire for centuries."

"What are you talking about? No, she hasn't. Not even ten years.

Really, for someone who's supposed to know so much, you're pretty dumb." Without another word, Sammi headed into the dorm room, leaving Rachael staring after her wondering what in the world was going on.

This wasn't the first time lately someone had told her something that didn't make sense, something that didn't match what she'd written. What in the world was going on? She had no idea, but she needed to talk to the one person who might be able to help her figure it out. Forgetting about the vampire bits all over her, Rachael headed into the dorm room and ran to the left instead of the right. She needed answers before those answers changed, too.

34

A SITUATION

Rachael

BANGING on the door got her nowhere for almost five minutes. Rachael's knuckles were hurting, and she imagined she'd woken anyone up who hadn't gone on the hunt. But she didn't care. She needed answers. And he was the only one who could give them to her--if anyone could.

When Jared finally made it to the door, it became clear as to why it had taken him so long to answer. He was wearing a towel--only a towel. And his hair was wet.

He pulled the door open and said, "Fuck, Rachael. What the hell?"

"Sorry," she muttered, though her eyes were a little busy tracing his chiseled chest, down to his waist and lower. The towel was slung pretty low, so low in fact she could start to see that perfect V form that would've gotten her mouth watering even if it wasn't a guy she had already made out with lots of times but never gotten to this point with.

"What's going on?"

Rachael looked around. A few doors were cracked, which let her know her frantic knocking had gotten her more attention than she'd wanted or realized. "Can I come in?"

"Yeah." He opened the door wider, and she stepped into his living room area, but the door didn't close all the way. That was fine with her. Less chance of her to get sidetracked by those abs--again.

"Listen, I'm sorry to bother you. I know I sound a little crazy right now. But the thing is... Sammi just told me something about Chell and Sasha that I didn't write."

Jared's eyebrows arched, but he didn't say anything at first, only stared at her. Eventually, he asked, "What do you mean?"

"I mean... I thought when I got here everything was parallel to what I'd written in my book. But that's not the case. I didn't write that Sasha and Chell had gone to high school together. In my book, Sasha was an ancient vampire, like, she'd been around for a super long time. But Sammi just told me that they went to high school together, that they were on the cheerleading squad together, and that Chell was there when Sammi got turned, and that's why Sasha was after her all the time."

Jared made sure his towel was fastened securely and then stroked his chin while he folded one arm under his elbow. "That's... interesting."

"Interesting--and crazy. What does it mean? If I wrote the world that collided with mine, or whatever it is we've thought happened, shouldn't everything be the same? There are other things that have been different, too. I didn't write Graham as the leader either. Who knows what else is weird."

"All right, Rachael, try to take some deep breaths, okay? There's got to be a logical explanation."

"There's not even a logical explanation for what we thought was going on to begin with, so how can there be one for this?" She ran her hands through her hair and nearly tugged a few strands out when she let go.

"Rachael, whatever it is, we'll get to the bottom of it. Maybe... the worlds didn't quite overlap."

"Or maybe there's a third world involved now, Jared, one neither one of us knows anything about. Maybe there's another writer out there now fucking with our lives."

He smirked at her, and that made Rachael's eyes bulge. "I'm sorry. I didn't mean to laugh at you. It's just... what you just said to me about Chell and Sasha isn't new to me. I already knew that. So... I don't think anything's changing right at the moment. I think you're panicking for no reason."

"If that's the case, why didn't you mention it to me?"

"Why would I? I can't think of any time it would've come up."

"I don't know--maybe when Sasha was trying to kill me. Or that other time, when Sasha was trying to kill me!"

He was trying not to laugh again. She could see it. "My point is, if I already knew about it, then maybe that's a good indicator that nothing has changed."

"Or it's a good indication that everything has changed, including what you think you've always known that a few days ago wasn't what you thought you knew at all!"

"That didn't even make sense, Rach!"

"It made perfect sense to me!"

He stepped toward her and put his hands on her arms, rubbing them slightly as he applied a bit of pressure. "Rachael, we don't need to figure this out right now. It's all right. It's going to be all right. Take some deep breaths in through your nose, out through your mouth, and try to calm down."

She did as he said, not because she agreed that it wasn't a reason to panic or that they didn't need to get to the bottom of it right that moment but because she had no other choice. It did help, though. She kept her eyes focused on Jared's and felt her pulse slowing.

"Are you okay?"

She nodded, afraid if she opened her mouth again, some sort of squeal would come out. Jared pulled her closer, and Rachael rested her head on his shoulder. "It'll be all right," he said, smoothing back her hair.

He smelled clean and fresh, and just a few weeks ago, she would've been backing him toward the couch, pulling that towel away. But...

things had changed in her universe, too, and she remembered she was supposed to be in her room with Graham.

She was just about to pull her head up and thank him when she heard Graham's voice behind her. "Well, this is awkward."

Rachael spun around quickly, catching his eyes. "No--it's not. I can explain."

Graham didn't say anything, only closed the door, and Rachael could hear his footsteps echoing down the hallway as he hurried away.

"Shit!"

"Let him go," Jared begged, pulling on her hand. "Come on, Rach. Don't chase him. He didn't even let you explain."

She turned to look at him. "I can't let him think something was happening that wasn't."

Jared gently pulled her toward him. "What if something was happening?"

That towel, slung so precariously around his hips, was all that was separating her from making a huge decision, one she had no idea she'd be faced with when she'd come running to him for help.

Rachael inhaled deeply and tried to pull her eyes back up to his, thinking of those lavender orbs and how much shock she'd seen in them as she'd turned to see Graham go.

She had a choice to make, all right, and not an easy one.

35

____

AWKWARD

Rachael

"I'VE GOTTA TO," Rachael told Jared as Graham's footsteps faded down the hall.

"You know, you really don't," he countered. "You could just stay here."

"Jared, please don't. We've been through all of this. Why would you want to do it all again?"

"Because I miss you. Because I want to be with you. Because I know even though you think you're in love with Graham, you miss me, too."

She narrowed her eyes at him. He was right--about all of it except one word. There was no "think" about it. He had solidified her answer. "I'll see you tomorrow."

She had to assume Graham had gone back to his own room, so she took off in that direction and caught up to him just as he was punching in his code to open the door. "Graham, wait. Listen, I went to Jared because of something Sammi said--something I thought he could explain."

"Did he insist you hug him while he was naked in order to get your answers?" Graham asked, the door cracked open. He could slip inside and be gone, and she wouldn't have time to follow. But he waited.

"No, that was just because he was doing his best to make me feel better about the entire situation."

"What situation?" Graham let the door go and turned to face her, his arms folded as he slumped against the door.

Rachael took a few steps forward but left a space between them because she didn't want to scare him away. "Things seem to be changing, Graham, in ways no one can explain. Remember earlier when you told me you were the leader, and I said I'd never written that?"

He nodded, raising an eyebrow but not moving yet.

"Well, I also didn't write the history between Chell and Sasha. I didn't write that they were human friends, that Sasha had been with Chell when she'd gotten turned. In my version, Sasha had been a vampire for a really long time before she even met Chell. I feel like, if you and Jared, and Sammi, and everyone else, had known there were inconsistencies, you would've said something. Which makes me think you're changing, too."

Graham studied her for a second and then let out a deep sigh. He dropped his arms and walked the few steps over to her, putting his hands on her lower arms. "Rachael, I can see why that would be upsetting. I don't have an explanation for it, but it's possible it just never came up. I don't know why our world would be mostly the same as what you wrote but not exactly the same. Maybe... whatever power you have that led you see into our reality wasn't as detailed as it needed to be for you to write your books, so you just had to fill in the blanks."

"Maybe." She shook her head and closed her eyes for a second. "But I don't think so. I feel like things are shifting again. That night when I was in the cemetery, and you came to talk to me, I felt the ground shift again, just slightly. Maybe that was something else, a new collision of worlds, and I'm just now starting to see there were changes."

"I don't know. The whole situation is bizarre. Until we can figure out how it is that you knew so much about us before you met us, we won't have any answers."

"And we don't seem to be getting any closer to figuring that out. I don't think Sasha is the key to finding the answers, but I can't concentrate on solving the mystery of the world's colliding while a vampire is trying to kill me."

"Just explode her head," he said with a shrug.

A grin pulled up the corner of her mouth. "I don't think that will work with someone as powerful as she is."

"How did you know it wouldn't work on us?"

"That's what Sammi asked me."

"Well, how did you know?"

"Lucky guess."

Graham wrapped his arms around her waist and tugged her closer with a power that caused her to tingle in all of the right places. The scent of him, fresh from the shower, clean, with a hint of soap, and spicy, had her pulse racing.

He ran a finger beneath her chin and lifted her face. Rachael met his eyes and bit her bottom lip, not sure what he was about to say but feeling in her blood it was enough to send her over the edge.

Leaning so close she could feel his warm breath on her neck, Graham said, "The next time you consider blowing my head, it better be the one in my pants."

Rachael's eyes widened, and Graham's lips devoured hers. That was a command she'd be glad to oblige.

TOGETHER AT LAST

Rachael

TAKING a shower was a necessity at this point, so Rachael headed straight for her bathroom, though the fact that Graham was waiting for her on the couch made her wish vampire guts came out of one's hair a lot easier than they did.

He'd been so naughty in the hallway, talking to her about blowing his head. Really--who said that if they weren't ready to get it on? But then, when she'd invited him into the shower with her, he'd passed, reminding her that he'd just taken a shower. Maybe she'd need a cold shower after all of this if he didn't mean what he'd just said.

He'd asked for her laptop, so she'd given it to him. She supposed he must be looking up some information about what she'd told him, though she knew there wouldn't be anything to be found in any of the files that would help, assuming nothing had changed there with all of this ground shaking and what-not.

Once she was fairly certain her hair was vampire-free, Rachael turned the water off and stepped out, drying off, putting on a pair of boy shorts and a camisole in a light blue she knew looked great on her, and brushed her teeth. Then, she hand dried her hair a little more before brushing it into a ponytail on top of her head. Hanging the towel to dry, she stepped out to see Graham still sitting on her couch, her laptop open in front of him.

He was studying it so closely he didn't hear her come out. Rachael slid onto the couch next to him. He turned and smiled at her but then did a double take. "Well, hello," he said, putting his arm around her. "You look nice. And smell great."

"Better than my vampire bits and pieces look?"

"Definitely." He ran his nose down the side of her cheek, igniting her flesh, and trailed his fingertips along the skin of her side. Rachael was tempted to close the laptop and climb onto his lap, but then the words at the top of the screen caught her attention.

"What did you find?"

"Not much. Just a few historical documents that relate to what you're saying. In 1854, a hunter reported an inconsistency in a vampire's backstory. Same thing happened in 1923."

It was the words "Inconsistent history" that had caught her attention. "So... do you think that was due to a world collision or something else--like vampires lying or being misreported?"

"I have no idea. But it's something we can do further research into. But not right now."

"Why not?" Rachael asked before she realized what he had in mind. Graham closed the laptop and pulled her over.

She complied, swinging her leg across him, her knee rubbing against him to let him know that her thoughts were on the same trajectory as his.

Her shirt had slid up slightly so his hands were on her skin at her midriff. She settled against him, thinking there were far too many layers of clothing in the way. As he began to kiss her, his tongue teased and tangled with hers, his hands gliding across her flesh. Rachael let out a soft moan, but then, she remembered this was not the first time they'd been in this position. In fact, this had happened more times than she could count. And then there was the night Jared had interrupted them when they were almost to the point of no return. As delicious as his lips were, she found herself pulling away.

"Graham, are you ready for this--or should we wait?"

He was fighting himself to keep from lunging for her lips--she could tell. "Wh--what?" he asked, his forehead crinkled.

"Look, we've been here a few times before, and I'm okay with just making out, or whatever you're comfortable doing, but if you already know you're not ready for more, I'd just as soon know that now."

Rather than answering her with words, Graham grabbed a hold of her bottom and pulled her up while standing. Rachael wrapped her legs around his waist, and he carried her to the bed, his mouth locked on hers.

If there had been any doubt in her mind that he was ready, that all faded away as he laid her down and stripped off his clothes, Rachael bit her bottom lip, watching him in anticipation. He came to her, pulling her shirt over her head and tugging her shorts off as well. Rachael had never been more certain of anything in her life than the idea that she and Graham were meant to be together.

He took his time, touching, caressing, kissing, sucking, working his way down her entire body, leaving her writhing and moaning before he finally grabbed hold of her hips and thrust into her, leaving her breathless and panting his name. For what might've been hours, he kept her at the peak of ecstasy, arching her back and grinding into him, his arms a solace she never wanted to breach. When he finally finished, Rachael rested against his chest, trying to recover but knowing, even if she woke up looking into the venomous eyes of a vampire in an hour's time, it would all be worth it to finally get to experience this ground shaking ride with Graham.

As she began to nod off, his warm breath on her ear roused her slightly. "I love you, Rachael. More than anything. More than anyone."

"I love you, too," she murmured, knowing his love was worth all of the insanity bringing him--and vampires--to life had caused. With Graham by her side, she knew everything was going to be all right, even if the world continued to shift and spin out of control. She'd find a way to put it all back together--one way or another.

DID EVERYTHING SHIFT?

Rachael

THE NEXT MORNING, Rachel fully expected the earth to have shifted again, not because another writer had caused two worlds to collide but because she'd finally consummated her relationship with Graham, and if anything should make the world shake, that should do it.

While things were different when she opened her eyes and saw him staring at her, nothing universally life-altering seemed to have taken place. He smiled, brushed some hair back from her face, and asked, "How are you?"

"Great," Rachael admitted, returning his grin. "How are you?"

His smile said it all. "I'm not sure why we waited so long to do that."

She knew exactly why but didn't feel like now was a good time to bring up his dead fiancé. "What do you have to do today?"

"I have some potential recruits I need to check on, but I think we both need to go sit down with Jared and see if we can come up with any explanation as to what it was I read online last night about this happening before, where pasts seemed to be altered with no reasonable explanation."

Rachael nodded. She'd been hoping he'd have some free time to do that. Now that her acceleration was over, she had no idea what her schedule would look like. "Doesn't he have classes today?"

"Yeah. I'll call him and see when we can come by."

"Won't that be a little odd after what happened last night?"

Graham made a face. "What do you mean?"

Shifting so she was looking at him more directly, Rachael reminded him, "You walked in on the two of us hugging, remember? And all he was wearing was a towel? I had to chase you down."

"Right. I remember that now. But... why would that make things awkward between him and me?"

She rolled her eyes, thinking, "Men," and collapsed back onto her pillow. "You guys didn't even talk about it."

"What is there to talk about? He was hitting on you and failed. I scored. We're good."

"You might think so, but that doesn't mean he will, especially if he realizes you spent the night here."

"I've spent the night here before and nothing has happened between us. No one will know for sure something did this time."

"Oh, they'll know," she begged to differ. "Besides, everyone else has already assumed that's the case. Now, they'll just have their confirmation."

"Listen, Rachael, if anyone starts treating you poorly because of me, you let me know, and I'll deal with it," he said as he gently stroked her cheek with his thumb. "Or, you can just explode their heads, and that will also take care of it." He chuckled, and she couldn't help but grin.

"I'm pretty sure I can't do that."

"But do they know that?"

"If they were there last night, they probably do. Sammi asked me about it after the hunt."

"Well, they won't know for sure. And if I were them, that's not a bet I'd be willing to make. Can she or can't she make my head explode? Let's not find out."

Rachael rolled up and leaned her head on her hand. "I already did that once. You want me to do it again?" She raised an eyebrow and gave him her naughtiest smile.

Graham replied, "Now, how could I ever resist that?" He leaned down and smothered her mouth with his, swiping the sheet that had been between them out of the way, and Rachael surrendered to his touch, relishing every moment that she was in his arms.

Later that afternoon, they found themselves sitting in Jared's office, across the desk from him while he studied the two cases Graham had found online the night before.

Jared stroked his chin and contemplated the situations. "Well, I certainly don't remember having read these before. I wonder if they also changed when Rachael noticed these new alterations in history or if we've just never paid attention to them because they never mattered before."

"This would be a lot easier if history didn't change--if we could go back to supporting documents and see what's the same and what's not, but there's no way to do that," Rachael lamented, mostly to herself.

"Not without locating the original realm," Jared pointed out. "If you could go back to the original, unaltered version of your realm, then you could compare."

"Wait--there's an original unaltered version of my previous reality?"

"Maybe," Jared said with a shrug. "I don't know how it works, but if there was, and you could cross back into it, then you'd know for sure."

"But... I don't know how I did this in the first place, and none of my attempts to do it again have worked."

"Right," Jared nodded. "I'm aware of the brick wall we've hit with that." He shrugged. "It looks like it's possible small pieces of history are changing still, but I don't know why."

"Small? I'd say Sasha's previous existence altering and none of us remembering the old version except Rachael is significant," Graham interjected. He'd been relatively quiet up until that moment, and when Jared glared at him, Rachael understood why. In spite of what he'd said earlier, he knew Jared wasn't happy with him.

"Okay--large, significant, however you want to put it. I've read and re-read my grandfather's book, all of his notes, everything we have, and I still have no idea how any of this is happening."

"Maybe there's something else in the library," Rachael suggested.

Jared was shaking his head before she even finished. "I've checked there."

"When?" Graham asked.

"I don't know. A few weeks ago."

"Well, if things are constantly changing, maybe we should check again." Rachael was out of her chair before either of them could respond.

"I've got a class to teach," Jared reminded them. "You two go ahead. I doubt you'll find anything, but if you come across something that seems at all plausible, let me know."

"All right. Thanks, Jared." Graham offered him his hand, and Jared shook it, which all seemed odd to Rachael considering they were friends, not two guys working out a business arrangement, but she said nothing and walked out with Graham, headed to the library. Hopefully, they'd find some answers there. If not, she had no idea where else to turn.

38

WHERE'S THE BOOK?

Rachael

THE MOMENT RACHAEL walked into the library, she knew something was different. It just didn't feel the same as it had the last time she was there. From what she could tell, the books were arranged in the same way, the sections in the same places, but it didn't seem to be exactly the same, and that left her hopeful.

She went straight to the place where she'd found Jared's grandfather's book and started checking for any new titles that hadn't stood out to her before. Graham did the same in another, similar section, pulling out any books that seemed like they might have some answers.

Rachael wasn't finding much. Only a couple of books looked like they might not have been there before, or she might have just missed them. Then, she saw a book she was almost certain hadn't been there before. The cover was leather, in brown and blue, and it looked new, like it had never been opened. She pulled it out and noticed the edges of the pages were all gold.

"Realms and Portals: Questions and Answers," she read aloud, gaining Graham's attention. He stopped over. "By William Barnes."

Her mouth dropped open, and she looked up to see a similar expression on Graham's face. "That's… your dad."

"I guess so." She flipped it over, but of course there was no "about the author" on the back cover like there would've been on a modern book. "Do you think this was here before?"

"No, I don't. Let's go see if it has any answers to our questions," Graham said, ignoring all of the other books they'd pulled and heading over to the seating area.

Rachael followed, folding her hands as she went. They were shaking a little. She sat down next to Graham, and he opened the book to the table of contents.

The book definitely held promise if the questions listed here were actually answered. "How Two Realms Collide, Our Changing Worlds, The Magic of a Realm Jumper, Writing Your Destiny." Graham read through all of the titles, and every single one of them seemed to hold some promise of explaining what was happening to her. The last chapter title caught her eye, too. "How to Find Your Way Home." Graham's eyes bore into hers. "Do you think… he's lost?"

"I do now," she admitted.

"Where shall we start?" Graham asked her, and Rachael wasn't sure what to say, so she just shrugged. "Okay. Chapter One: How Two Realms Collide."

For hours, the two of them sat there on the sofa reading a book apparently penned by her missing father, which seemed to explain exactly what was going on, how Rachael had ended up there, why her father had been missing from her life, and potentially how to fix all of it. While some of the solutions were similar to ones Rachael had tried before, they weren't exactly the same. She needed to modify her approach to writing changes if any of them were to work, and it seemed like there was no way she could bring the Chell that died in this realm back to life, but there was the possibility they could locate a similar Chell in another realm and bring her here--if she wanted to come.

"I don't want to do that," Graham noted before Rachael even asked. "If there's a Chell in another realm, there could well be a Graham that loves her."

"What if there isn't?" Rachael asked.

He shrugged. "She's still not my Chell."

Rachael offered him a sympathetic smile. "Okay--we need to go talk to Jared," she said. "Now that we know what can be changed, maybe he can help us understand how to change it."

"What is it exactly you want to change, though?" Graham asked her.

Rachael wasn't sure. "All I know is, I want the world to stop changing by itself. And I want to find my dad. And stop Sasha."

"Great--that all sounds good to me. The only thing is, the world isn't changing by itself. Someone is changing it. We just don't know who. We might be able to find your dad, but as far as Sasha is concerned, I don't think the answer to that is in the book."

"You don't?" Rachael felt her shoulders slumping. "Why not?"

"Because that's just old school vampire hunting."

She knew he was right about that. Rachael took a deep breath. "So... we essentially just need to find out who is changing the world right now and get him or her to stop it?"

"I think so. And find your dad."

"And find my dad...."

"The fact that he got this book here makes me think he's got to be close."

She nodded. "Assuming he got it here."

"Who else could've done that?"

"I don't know. But it could be whoever is writing the changes now."

"True. Well, first things first. Let's go talk to Jared, and see what he thinks."

Rachael nodded and stood, taking Graham's hand. Before they got too far, she tugged him back. "Thanks for all of your help, Graham."

"You're welcome, babe." He smiled at her, and she stretched up on her tiptoes and planted a kiss on his lips. They might not have any solutions yet, but they were far closer to them than they had been when they'd first entered the library, and Rachael finally felt like she was getting somewhere, even if they still had a long way to go.

3 9

A TOOL

Rachael

"THIS IS EXTREMELY INTERESTING," Jared said, holding the book in his hands. "It's particularly compelling that it's written, apparently, by Rachael's father. But I'll have to read through it before I can know for sure what it tells us."

"Right," Graham agreed. "We read through a lot of it, but not the whole thing. So far, it's got a lot of great information, but it doesn't tell us what we need to do. Or even necessarily why this is happening now."

"It seems like someone is writing, someone with the power to change things," Rachel noted.

"But why would they want to change something as meaningless as Sasha's background?" Jared asked.

Graham shrugged. "Maybe that's just a product of whatever the writer is trying to change that is important. I have no idea."

"Okay--leave the book with me, and I'll see what I can figure out," Jared suggested.

Rachael didn't really want to do that. She wanted to take the book with her so she could continue to read it herself, but since Jared was more likely to be able to make heads or tails out of the writing, she decided to let it go. "Thanks," she said, letting out a deep breath.

"In the meantime, we need to get on this clan that's starting to form in Hagerstown," Jared said, typing something into his laptop before he spun it around for them to see. "Two attacks in three days. The group seems to be getting bigger all the time."

"Is it just me, or does it seem like there are suddenly more vampires than there were a few days ago, too?" Rachael asked, wondering if this was a part of what was going on or something else.

"Could be a result of Sasha trying to grow her army," Graham said with a shrug.

"Or it could be another world coming in that is actually more densely populated than the world we are used to," Jared suggested.

"Does that not bother you?" They both seemed so nonchalant about the entire situation.

"At the moment, it doesn't seem to be more than we can handle," Graham replied. "If they start to get out of hand, then we'll reevaluate."

"Well, you might wanna put your recruiting efforts into overtime," Rachael said, looking at Graham.

He nodded, as if he understood why she would say that. "Let us know what you figure out, Doc." He gave Jared a half-smile and headed out of his office. Rachael followed, not sure what else she could do.

Something about Jared's reaction to the book was concerning to her, though. He seemed lackadaisical about the whole thing, like it wasn't a big deal. Later, lying in bed next to Graham in the middle of the afternoon, Rachael stared up at the ceiling and tried to put the situation into perspective.

"Are you okay?" Graham asked, brushing her arm with his fingertips.

"Yeah. It's just… Jared seemed to already know about that book, didn't he?"

"Did he?" Graham asked, his eyebrows furrowing.

"Yeah, I think so. He didn't seem nearly as surprised to see it as we did."

"Huh. Maybe he just assumed it had to exist."

"And that my dad had written it?"

"Yeah, I don't know," Graham admitted, kissing her bare shoulder. "Jared's an odd fellow."

"I guess so." She was beginning to think Jared expected them to find the book. Maybe he'd even seen it before. She just hoped it didn't disappear. "I wish there'd been more information about how to find my dad," she noted.

"Me, too. Maybe he'll find that. I know you'll feel better when you can talk to Billy and see if he can explain exactly where he's been all of these years."

Rachael nodded and rested her head on his shoulder. Her entire life, she'd been led to believe that her dad had just walked out on her and her mom, that he just left them to go do something he felt was more important or more fun than taking care of his family. Now, she thought perhaps she'd been wrong this whole time, and he'd actually been straddling two realities and couldn't come back.

Graham's phone dinged on the nightstand next to her. She grabbed it and handed it to him, and he checked the text. "We're going on a hunt in an hour," he said.

"Who called that?" Rachael was confused. She thought Graham was in charge of all the hunts now.

"Tripp. He's organizing it. I just approved it."

"Oh." That made more sense. For a moment, she thought everything had shifted again.

"Okay. Am I going?"

"Of course you are. We need your superpowers," he replied.

Rachael chuckled and kissed his cheek, glad she had proven herself worthy of the team. Whatever was going on with the shifting reality would have to wait until later. For now, they had vampires to hunt down and destroy. At least that was becoming routine and shouldn't be anything out of the ordinary.

4 0

———

WHO WAS THAT GIRL?

Rachael

Unlike the other hunts Rachael had been on, this one did not involve a dilapidated house that looked like it was about to fall over. No, this one was more like Frank's house. Except there was no furniture in it. Not a scrap. There was a for sale sign outside, though, which told her that vampires were not above squatting in houses that sat on the market too long.

It was a small group tonight since the report had been a lone male vampire seen slinking into the home the last few nights. Rachael was glad Sammi hadn't gone with them. Neither had Marcy. She was the only woman--just her, Graham, Jared, Tripp, and Ty. All the way over, they'd been a bunch of dudes, listening to loud music, using language they never would've if there'd been other women present. But Rachael had insisted after Tripp's first slip up it was fine, so they were clearly enjoying themselves. Rachael felt like she had been sucked into a road trip with a group of bros.

The house was a two-story, and she was assigned to go in the back door with Jared. Graham and Ty would go in the front, and Tripp was

181

coming in from the roof. It was different than they normally operated since the entire team hadn't come along. Rachael wasn't sure if the others decided not to come because she was there or if they had other plans. All she knew was she was glad she was there and couldn't care less what they'd been thinking.

"How are you feeling?" Jared asked as he unlocked the back door with just the touch of his hand.

"Good," she assured him. "Excited." She was a little surprised Graham had assigned her to Jared, but he obviously trusted her, as he should.

Jared nodded and then opened the door. He slowly stepped inside, and Rachael followed, noting they were in a poorly lit kitchen. Obscured by mature trees, the windows didn't let in much light. Only the glow from the clock on the microwave and a small stream of light coming from underneath an adjoining door lit their path.

"Got him," Tripp said quietly. "Master bedroom occupied once."

"Is he up and about or sleeping?" Graham asked, and Rachael could hear his voice on the stairs.

"He's night," Tripp replied. Rachael stifled a laugh at his choice of words. "He's about to go bye."

The sound of metal and wood tearing through flesh and bone would've made Rachael gag in her normal life, but now, it was the sound of victory, and it didn't bother her at all.

"That's done," Tripp replied, no longer whispering.

Jared looked disappointed. "Well, that didn't take long."

"Sorry," Rachael said, giving him a sympathetic smile. She was also disappointed. It would've been nice to use her powers again. She could feel her palms practically itching to blow something--or some-one--up.

A strange noise emanated from beneath the door where the light was glowing. The two hunters exchanged glances, and Jared took a few steps closer. The sound of the others walking around upstairs, as loudly as they wanted since they were all under the impression the hunt was over, made Rachael look up as Jared pushed the door open.

It was a laundry room, and it appeared to be empty. He stepped in, and Rachael followed. The light was on, revealing a few old boxes she assumed the people who'd left hadn't wanted to take with them. That was it, besides a few cabinets attached to the wall, including one that was large enough to house brooms and mops. Jared kicked at one of the boxes, and they heard the noise again.

"Rats," he said with a shrug.

"Figures." Rachael looked around, feeling a little unsettled.

"Hey, want me to lure him out, and you can see if your abilities to blow up heads apply to rodents?"

The idea of making a rat's head explode didn't sound too appealing to Rachael. "No thanks," she said, shaking her head.

"Ah, why not? It's better than letting him starve to death in an empty house that has no food." Jared kicked the box again, his back to the cabinets, and this time, Rachael swore she heard something move behind him.

"Jared?"

"Come on out, little ratty, ratty, ratty," he called.

"Jared...."

He kicked the box once more. It tumbled over, and as he began to laugh at the pair of rats that took off scurrying across the floor, the large cabinet doors behind him flew open.

A woman came rushing out, running into Jared and knocking him face first onto the floor. Rachael shrieked and threw her hands up, but the woman wasn't waiting for anyone. She charged at Rachael, her wild blonde hair blowing in her own wind as she tried to get out the only exit.

It wasn't until she was right on Rachael that she got a good look at the face. The fangs caught her attention first. As if it wasn't obvious that this was a vampire from her movement and the fact she'd been hiding from them, it was clear now. But that wasn't what left Rachael staring wide eyed, her mouth agape.

She recognized the woman rushing at her, the one that hissed in her face, pushed her aside, and ran straight for the nearest window, shattering the glass into a thousand pieces as she took off into the night.

Rachael covered her mouth, still trying to explain what she'd seen as Jared picked himself up off the floor. "Why didn't you get her, Rach?" he asked, dusting himself off.

"I... uh... it...." she stammered. Rachael shook her head, trying to clear her thoughts, staring from Jared to the broken window as the approaching footsteps reached them.

"What's the matter, Rachael?" Jared asked.

She looked into Graham's eyes as he came to stand beside her, and Rachael finally managed to explain, "It was... Chell."

Thank you for reading! Book 3 is coming soon!

ALSO BY ID JOHNSON

Stand Alone Titles
<u>All I Want for Christmas is Pooch</u>
(<u>*sweet contemporary romance*</u>)
<u>Christmas Memory</u>
(<u>*sweet contemporary romance*</u>)
<u>Meet Cute Me Under the Mistletoe</u>
(<u>*sweet contemporary romance*</u>)
<u>The Doll Maker's Daughter at Christmas</u>
(*clean romance/historical*)
<u>Pretty Little Monster</u>
(*young adult/suspense*)
<u>The Journey to Normal: Our Family's Life with Autism</u> (*nonfiction*)
<u>Found by the Alpha (fantasy romance)</u>

Love Throughout Time
(*time travel romance*)
Back to Titanic
Back to Gettysburg
Back to Bunker Hill

Back to the Highlands
Back to Port Royal

Silverwood Academy
(paranormal romance)
Vampire Hunter
World Builder
Realm Jumper

Celestial Springs
(psychological thriller/literary fiction/women's fiction)
Beneath the Inconstant Moon
The First Mrs. Edwards
Leaving Ginny

The Motherhood
(dystopian romance)
Rain's Rebellion
Rain's Run
Rain's Return

Ashes and Rose Petals
(contemporary romance/retelling of Romeo and Juliet and Cinderella)
Girl in the Attic
Girl From the Tomb
Girl On the Beach

Nashville Country Dreams
(contemporary romance)
Meant to Marry Me
Lead Me Home
You Are the Reason

Forever Love series

(clean romance/historical)
<u>Cordia's Will: A Civil War Story of Love and Loss</u>
<u>Cordia's Hope: A Story of Love on the Frontier</u>

The Clandestine Saga series
(paranormal romance)
<u>Transformation</u>
<u>Resurrection</u>
<u>Repercussion</u>
<u>Absolution</u>
<u>Illumination</u>
<u>Destruction</u>
<u>Annihilation</u>
<u>Obliteration</u>
<u>Termination</u>

A Vampire Hunter's Tale (based on The Clandestine Saga)
(paranormal/alternate history)
<u>Aaron</u>
<u>Jamie</u>
<u>Elliott</u>
<u>Christian</u>

The Chronicles of Cassidy (based on The Clandestine Saga)
(young adult paranormal)
<u>So You Think Your Sister's a Vampire Hunter?</u>
<u>Who Wants to Be a Vampire Hunter?</u>
<u>How Not to Be a Vampire Hunter</u>
<u>My Life As a Teenage Vampire Hunter</u>
<u>Vampire Hunting Isn't for Morons</u>
<u>Vampires Bite and Other Life Lessons</u>
<u>Gone Guardian</u>
<u>Death Does Not Become Her</u>

Blood of the Vampire Hunter (based on The Clandestine Saga)
(paranormal romance)
<u>Night Slayer</u>
<u>Shadow Stalker</u>
<u>Queen Catcher</u>
<u>Mother Hunter</u>
<u>Father Finder</u>

Ghosts of Southampton series
(historical romance)
<u>Prelude</u>
<u>Titanic</u>
<u>Residuum</u>
<u>Lusitania</u>

Heartwarming Holidays Sweet Romance series
(Christian/clean romance)
<u>Melody's Christmas</u>
<u>Christmas Cocoa</u>
<u>Winter Woods</u>
<u>Waiting On Love</u>
<u>Shamrock Hearts</u>
<u>A Blossoming Spring Romance</u>
<u>Firecracker!</u>
<u>Falling in Love</u>
<u>Thankful for You</u>
<u>Melody's Christmas Wedding</u>
<u>The New Year's Date</u>

Charles Town Brides (based on Heartwarming Holidays Sweet Romance)
(Christian/clean romance)
<u>From This Moment</u>
<u>Can't Help Falling in Love</u>
<u>It's Your Love</u>

When You Say Nothing At All
My Girl
Unchained Melody
I Only Have Eyes For You
At Last
The Very Thought of You

Reaper's Hollow
(*paranormal/urban fantasy*)
Ruin's Lot
Ruin's Promise
Ruin's Legacy

When Kings Collide
(*steamy historical romance*)
Princess of Silence
Princess of Hearts

Collections
Ghosts of Southampton Books 0-2
Reaper's Hollow Books 1-3
The Clandestine Saga Books 1-3
The Chronicles of Cassidy Books 1-4
Celestial Springs Collection
Heartwarming Holidays Sweet Romance Books 1-3
Heartwarming Holidays Sweet Romance Books 4-7

Websites: https://books2read.com/ap/xX7ZD8/ID-Johnson

For updates, visit www.authoridjohnson.blogspot.com

Follow on Twitter @authoridjohnson

Find me on Facebook at www.facebook.com/IDJohnsonAuthor

Instagram: @authoridjohnson

Follow me on Bookbub: https://www.bookbub.com/authors/id-johnson

9 7 9 8 8 9 8 7 1 0 3 1 6